THE
DEADLIEST RETURNS

THE
DEADLIEST RETURNS

A COLLECTION OF MIRIAM BAT ISAAC NOVELETTES

JUNE TROP

First published by Level Best Books/Historia 2024

This novel is entirely a work of fiction. The names, characters and incidents portrayed in it are the work of the author's imagination. Any resemblance to actual persons, living or dead, events or localities is entirely coincidental.

Author Photo Credit: Photo copyright is owned by Michael Gold of The Corporate Image

First edition

ISBN: 978-1-68512-585-1

Cover art by Level Best Designs

This book was professionally typeset on Reedsy.
Find out more at reedsy.com

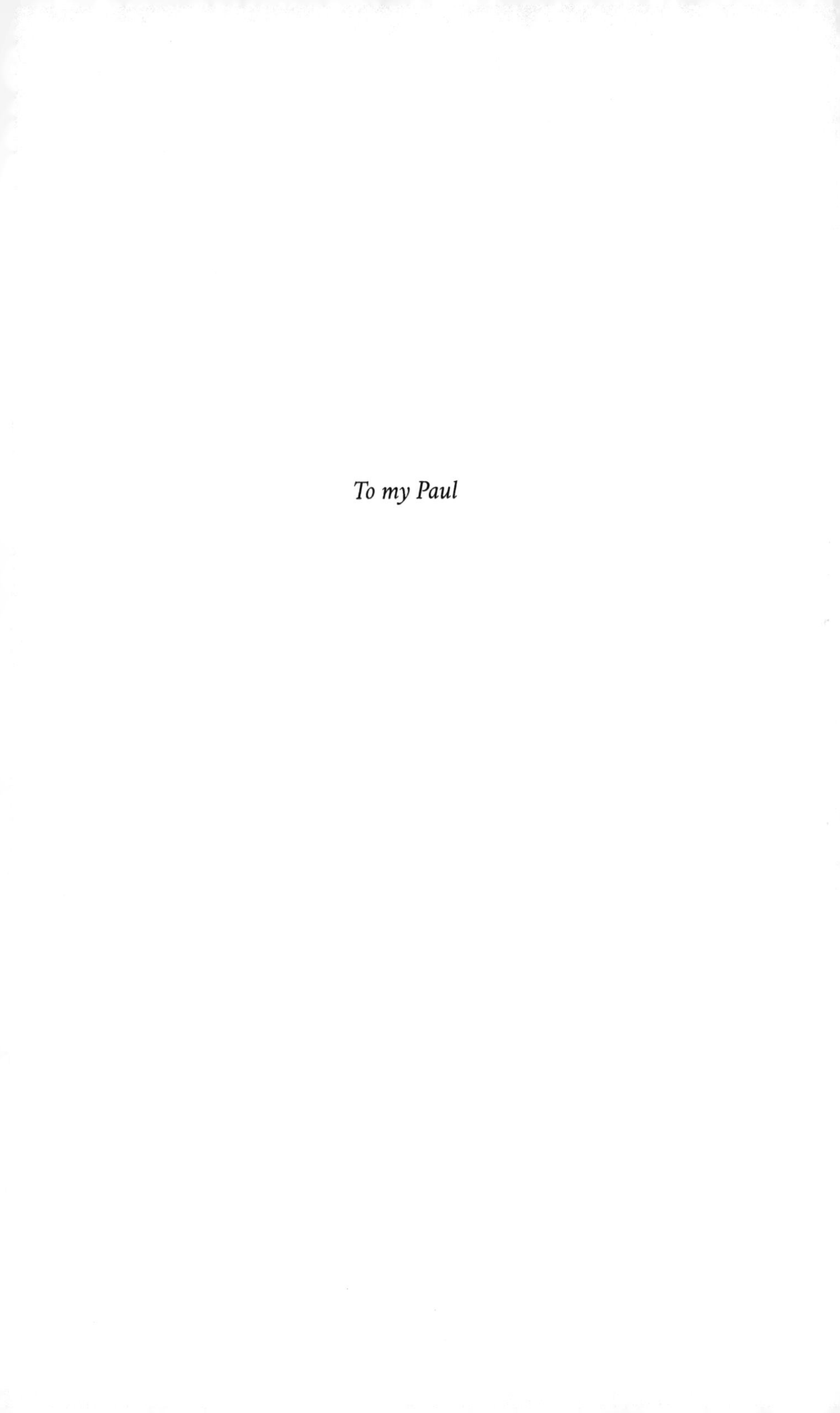

To my Paul

Contents

Praise for The Miriam bat Isaac Mysteries

"You've come through again with another brilliant volume…. Your writing is mind boggling, and the life you create, even dealing with the mysteries and horror of death, explode with a tremendous energy….You are presenting a gift to your readers, spellbinding them with historical settings filled with mysteries."—The Amazing Kreskin

Illustrations

MAP OF ALEXANDRIA

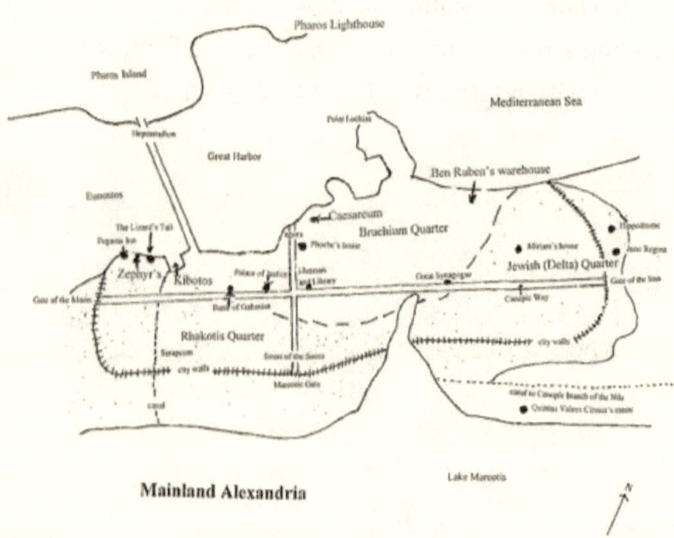

Adapted with permission from Sly, D. L. (1996). Philos' Alexandria. London: Routledge

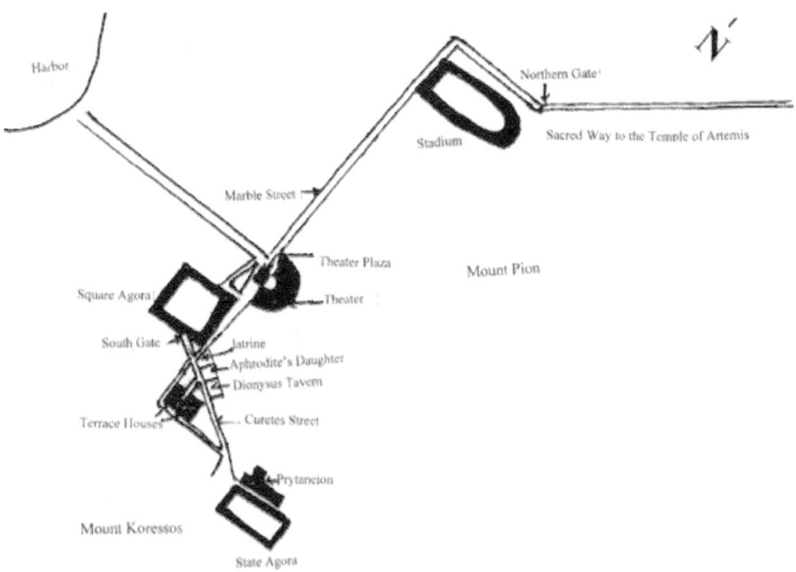

Miriam's Map of Central Ephesus

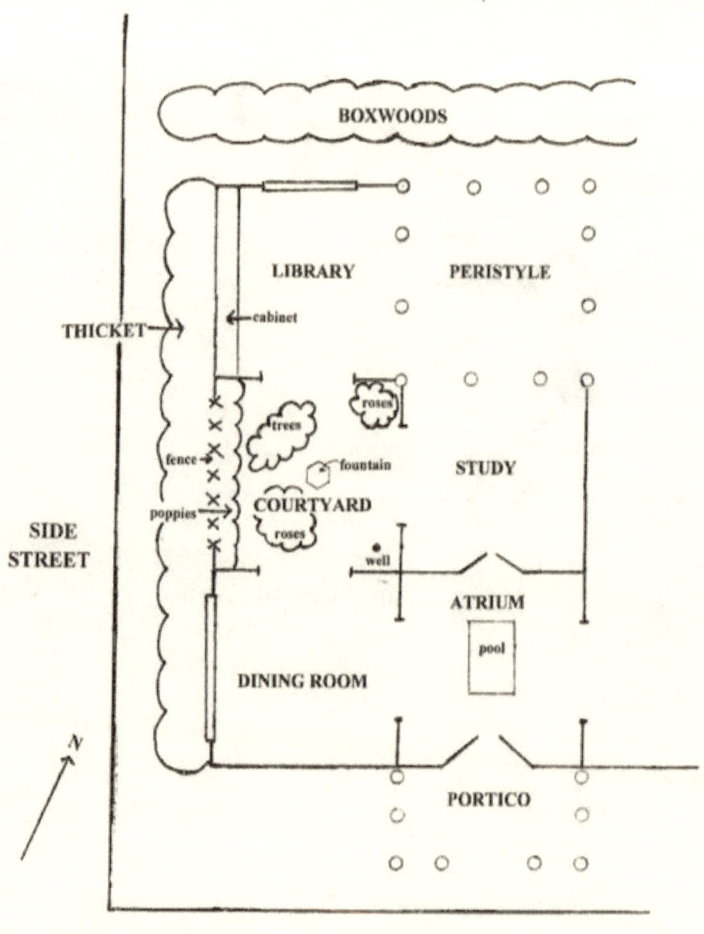

Miriam's House: Public Rooms

Miriam's House: Public Rooms

Introduction

Returning, whether it means going back or giving back, is never easy, at least not in this volume of three Miriam bat Isaac stories. In the first, "The Bodyguard," Miriam's brother, an erstwhile gladiator, returns home to continue serving as bodyguard to the son of a legionnaire who retires to Alexandria. In the second, "The Beggar," an old man posing as a beggar returns to Alexandria to find out the fate of the lovechild he left behind when he fled to escape the wrath of Roman law. And in the third, "The Black Pearl," Miriam, upon coming into possession of the cache of jewels heisted from the Temple of Artemis, sails with her husband to Ephesus to return the treasure. If, like Miriam, you thrive on pursuing the twists and turns of a baffling mystery while uncovering the guilty longings, secrets, lies, and evil deeds of others, then, as Miriam's deputy, you will have ample opportunity to engage your curiosity.

And if you are new to Roman-occupied Alexandria during the first century CE, you will experience, along with the splendor of the city, its malignant underbelly. You will blunder through its haunted alleys and wend your way through its shrill parade of macabre creatures. At the same time, the stench of each tumbling tenement and the scratch of every whirling piece of trash will coat the back of your throat with bile. And if you have never been to Ephesus, the capital of the Roman province of Asia, never seen the Temple of Artemis, one of the seven wonders of the Ancient World, then prepare yourself for the glassy heat of that July summer and the unnerving sight that will turn your celebratory visit into a mystifying tragedy.

Each adventure stands alone. Still, I recommend you read the stories in order. They are connected chronologically such that an event from an earlier story forms the backdrop for a later story. In any case, escape the monotony of everyday life as you accompany Miriam on three of her most daring exploits and find your way to truth and justice.

June Trop

I

The Bodyguard

The Tenth Year of the Reign of
Nero Claudius Caesar Augustus Germanicus [Nero]
64 CE, July
Alexandria ad Aegyptum

Characters

- **Abasi** courier who delivered the pouch to the Quintus Valens Cinnus household
- **Binyamin** Miriam's twin brother and ex-gladiator a.k.a. **Aquila** and **Agrippa Fortitudo**
- **Bion** Phoebe's husband and expert on analyzing documents
- **Calisto** Miriam's personal maid
- **Drusa** wife of Quintus Valens Cinnus
- **Gershon ben Israel** old friend of Binyamin's father
- **Judah** Miriam's husband and professional jeweler
- **Miriam** amateur sleuth extraordinaire
- **Orestes and Solon** Miriam's bearers
- **Phoebe** Miriam's best friend, erstwhile slave, Miriam's sleuthing partner
- **Professor Jason** medical school physician who investigates mysterious deaths
- **Quintus Valens Cinnus** retired legionnaire, Professor Jason's best friend, Drusa's husband
- **Sergius** ex-gladiator, Binyamin's friend and sponsor
- **Tullus** disabled son of Drusa and Quintus Valens Cinnus

Chapter One: Aquila (aka Binyamin)

The old fart's eyes were drilling into me. I shouldn't have risked coming. The games were a bore anyways. I was tired of the wild beast hunts and the roar of spectators whenever a gladiator's ass hit the sand. And right then, I was sick of those lice-infested clowns, the *praegenarii*, and the clack of their wooden swords as they mocked the gladiators with their corny antics. Besides, the sun was pricking through the awning of the hippodrome, staring down at me, coating my throat with dust. Time to hit a snack bar.

I joined the stream of bozos funneling through the arch, taking advantage of the break between bouts, most to push their way to the latrines. Shoving past the bookmakers wigwagging to their regulars, I carved my way around the hundreds of sweaty bodies milling about the souvenir hawkers. Finally, I elbowed through the gate and headed toward the sausage vendors. Their stalls were easy to find; they stunk up the air with fennel and fried grease.

Hey, I asked myself, *why not just leave after I grab a bite?* I'd seen enough of the *ludus* of Alexandria, the dinkiest gladiator school in the empire, and its lousy troupe of gladiators to last more than a life—

Whoa! That shitty geezer was right on my tail, sharking toward me. I cursed myself over and over for coming, but when I wanna do something, I gotta do it. That's the way I am. Now that I was back in Alexandria, I was that kid again, skipping school to sneak off to the games. The gladiators were like gods to me then, flexing their well-oiled muscles in the early morning light. And how I thrilled to those waves and applause when I was a *retiarius*, the kind of gladiator to fight with only a net and trident. No helmet. That was so Claudius, that prick, could watch our faces when our throats were cut. Anyways, my *lanista*, the manager of my troupe of gladiators, said I was too handsome to fight with a helmet.

"Agrippa, Agrippa Fortitudo!"

His voice pierced my eardrums like an icepick. Agrippa Fortitudo was my tag as a gladiator. That's what I meant about taking a risk. I was supposed to have been killed in the arena eight years ago.

Panic mushroomed in my chest. He was close enough for his shallow breath to foul the back of my neck. I tried to ignore him, but if he continued to shriek, a crowd would gather, and worse yet, draw one of those shit-eating soldiers. No way was that prune-puckered dude gonna leave me alone. Sure enough, a moment later he was poking me between my shoulder blades. So, I turned around and pitched him a scowl.

Ma Zeus, I knew him! Underneath that receding cap of silver curls was the moth-eaten version of Gershon ben Israel, aglitter with gems, reeking from verbena, and draped in a gaudy silk robe. A phony if I ever saw one. Another of Papa's ass-kissing buddies, all of them full of crap, just like my dear departed father.

"Sir, you must be mistaken. My name is Aquila—"

"Say again?" His head springing forward like a turtle's, he squeezed together the wrinkles across his forehead and cupped his ear.

That's when I remembered the *Khamaseen* winds, those hot, sand-filled windstorms that blow across Egypt in the spring. They must have burned out most of his hearing. With a furrowed brow, I threw up my hands and shook my head as if bewildered.

But he just took my hands and leaned into me. "Don't you remember me?"

I snapped my head back as if he'd struck me. Oh yeah, I can ham it up better than any of those sissy actors, Thespis included. Just one of the many tricks I'd learned to deflect my father's wrath.

"Who me, Papa?" I'd say, dropping my voice and blinking my eyes like a shitty cave dweller. "You think I did what? Jumped out the window to relieve my lust with Zenon's daughter? Where? In the pantry of her father's cookshop? How could that be? I was right here studying geometry. Honest." Then I'd shake my head and tighten my lips as if to hold back a moan of pity. That fuckin' tyrant wouldn't even send me to a *collegium iuvenum* to study martial arts. Oh no, he wanted me to learn the family business so I could waste my life counting money like him.

"Don't you remember me?" Gershon repeated. His voice had dropped to a croak. "And even if *you* don't, I remember when you were just a little-known contender about to be pitted against...uh...uh... Orcus! Yes, Orcus, the betting favorite and most popular gladiator in the empire."

I had to hand it to Gershon. He was a fucker-upper, fuckin' up my plan because that's what a fucker-upper does, but he was also an aficionado. And Orcus? He may have been the favorite, but he'd never faced *me*. That sucker, not a slave, prisoner a' war, or criminal but a hire like me, was just hours away from freedom, fighting his last bout before the contract with his *ludus* ended. Round and round we went: the flight of my net, the thrust of his sword. Me pressing every minute to my advantage until he was worn out. Then my net flew one last time. He couldn't escape. When his legs got caught, I closed in with my trident. The stadium suddenly, eerily silent, the fans stunned as I got the nod to plunge my *pugio* into his chest.

I was about to laugh like a hyena when, springing out of that memory, I realized I'd better do something about Gershon before he ruined everything.

* * *

Okay, so I was gonna have to tell that busybody something. Raising my palm to silence him and then beckoning him with a couple of arm rolls, he accompanied me to that teahouse near the Gate of the Sun, the *Juno Regina*. I figured anyone with any breath left would still be at the games. Besides, by now my throat was lined with sandpaper, and my lips were making a popping sound whenever I opened my mouth.

So, he shambled along while I *tsk-tsked*, shaken by how much that fogy had aged. All I saw was a lumbering old man with sagging jowls, a swinging dewlap, and a forward stoop, panting to keep up as we followed the curve of the city wall to the plaza with the teahouse.

Kicking aside eddies of trash and a dozing loafer slumped in a puddle of shade across the threshold, I peeked inside. Gershon wasn't the only thing to have hit the skids. The *Juno Regina* was now just a graffiti-scarred courtyard smothered in the heat with a cracked mudbrick floor, a tattered canopy, and scattered planters of dried-out pomegranate trees. Oh yeah, I almost forgot to mention the army of flies feasting on a counter of rancid cheese, moldy sesame cakes, and shriveled grapes.

Good enough. The place was deserted. Extending my hand to invite Gershon to enter, I pointed first with my chin to a table in the corner and then with my finger toward its far chair. Now that I'm in Alexandria, I sit with my back to the entrance to avoid having to tear a new asshole in every bozo who recognizes me. Come to think of it, I should have done that to this old goat. Instead, I had to watch him rub his palm across the seat of the chair, arrange the folds of his robe, sit down like a pussy, and smooth away the wrinkles in his skirt.

I rapped my knuckles on the table and then joggled—and almost broke—the branch off one of those stinking trees while shouting for service. All I wanted was a krater of honey-sweetened wine—anything but pomegranate! Ha!—and plenty of it. A dough-faced boy with constantly moving eyes and wearing the gray, coarse woolen tunic of a slave shuffled over and bowed like we were in Nero's palace. I gave him the order and told him to make it snappy, whatever good that would do.

Gershon started screeching right away. "What are you doing here? You were killed in Pompeii!"

I patted the air to calm him.

It didn't work.

"Your sister had an honorable burial for you with mimes, musicians, and professional mourners. She commissioned an everlasting monument to you in the Jewish cemetery not far from here—"

For each point, he jabbed his bony forefinger at me as if that deed alone should have made me dead.

"Inscribed with your record as a gladiat—"

"Listen," I said. I could hear the desperation in my voice over the sound of my heart as it punched the inside of my chest like a pointed rock.

He leaned across the table close enough to make my nose itch. But when he cupped one of his useless ears, I knew he was ready to shut up and listen.

"It's all been a mistake. I can explain. Right now, I got a job as a bodyguard, a good job I'm not about to blow. And I know I'm gonna have to tell my sister I'm here. And that's where you come in. When the time is right, you can help. So, you gotta keep my secret a while."

When he stroked his jaw with his thumb, I knew I had him.

Chapter Two: Miriam

"You're trembling, Calisto." I was addressing my sloe-eyed housemaid as she entered my study. Her hands were shaking like leaves in the wind. "And why are you bringing me wine instead of tea this early in the morning?"

My forefinger had been sliding down a column of numbers in the scroll with our mortgage holdings. Like my late father, I was attending to our family's investments behind the great ebony desk that used to be his. The bronze pen that had belonged to my mother was poised in my other hand, borrowing its feeble glow from the gray light of dawn brushing the columns of the peristyle behind me.

"Sorry, Miss Miriam," she answered, humility in the bow of her head. "Mr. Gershon's bearers just dropped off a message for you."

"So, why are you trembling?"

Before answering, her body stiffened under her coarse woolen tunic. "When I took the tablet from Wasi—maybe it was Wedu—You know I get the twins mixed up even though one of them has that scar like a fishhook wriggling down his cheek—"

"That's Wedu."

"Yes, well, when I took the tablet from—I guess it was Wasi—he said, 'Mr. Gershon wants you to bring Miss Miriam a goblet of wine before you give her this, and make sure she drinks all of it.'"

I could hear the fear clotting her voice.

"Well, I guess I better do it then," I said, shrugging with a pretense of nonchalance. I slipped my fingers through the goblet handles, swirling the wine, watching it spin, and breathing in its fruity scent. Then I took a few genteel sips, never taking my eyes off Calisto. Its warmth spread through my chest, returning my breakfast porridge with a soft belch.

"A little more," she ordered with the authority of a nurse.

I tipped the last of it down my throat with a sigh and replaced the goblet on the tray with a clink. "So, are you going to give me that tablet now?"

"Yes, Miss Miriam. Right away."

I stood waiting with crossed arms, looking around, feeling perplexed as if I was supposed to remember something.

Holding the tablet at a distance like a hissing serpent, she handed it to me with a question in her eye, but after a quick shake of my head, she dropped her gaze and withdrew.

I brought it into the peristyle to take advantage of the trapezoid of light the morning sun had painted on the stone floor. There I broke through Gershon's seal, untied the leather bands around the wooden frame, and opened the tablet to its waxed surface.

Try as I might, I could make no sense of the characters impressed in the wax. I managed to hang onto a word or two, but then the sentence wandered off on its own. Was this some kind of joke? While looking up, rubbing my eyes, and stopping to consider what this absurdity could mean, I heard the thud of footsteps along our side street, the rustle of fine fabric, and a pair of arms paddling through the boxwood hedges beyond the peristyle. The steps drew nearer and louder along with the roar of blood rushing in my ears.

I turned toward the sound. A shadowy, broad-shouldered figure, his forearms ringed with gold bracelets, strode into the peristyle. Standing rigid, I took in a single breath to call for help, but something familiar sealed my mouth as I stared at the apparition before me. I must have fainted because in what seemed like a moment later—I really don't know how long—I saw the ghost of my dead brother bending over me. Propping my head up with one arm, he held in his other hand an amphora that flooded my nostrils with the bitter scent of sea salt.

* * *

When the fog around me lifted, I heard the ghost say, "Sis, it's me. Binny!"

"Binny? How could that be?" I murmured. But when I gripped his arm to sit up and felt the muscles and sinews of an athlete, I knew his presence was corporeal.

While he carried me into my study and set me down in one of my *curule* chairs, I grappled with this tangible form of him against the backdrop of that terrible day eight years ago. That was the day when Sergius, his brows rammed together, brought the news that death had claimed Binyamin in the Amphitheatre of Pompeii and that the ship bearing his sealed coffin had just docked in Alexandria. As if to reassure me, he reported that Binyamin died fearlessly, with pride in the glory of Rome. And so, the time had come for me to keep the promise I'd made to my brother when he joined his second *ludus*, the one in Alexandria. I paid for his body, held a splendid funeral for him at the Great Synagogue, and despite my distress over his career choice, commissioned Sergius to erect a monument to honor his accomplishments. Then, in the blur of these intervening years, it came to seem as if my brother had hardly existed at all.

This stunning return to Alexandria was actually Binyamin's second homecoming. He'd first left for Capua at sixteen, full of the hopes and dreams of every young man. He was ready to satisfy the blood lust of the empire and fight with the desperation that attended his growing up in a family where he could do nothing right.

* * *

On the day he left for the pier to take his ship to Ostia, I'd hired a litter to take Binyamin and me there in style. I remember its fittings like molten gold under the baking sun, the polished ebony bodies of its eight Nubian bearers resplendent in their starched white tunics threaded with gold. Dizzy with the prospect of gliding through the streets high above the ox dung, I could pretend that we'd be riding on the wings of Mercury. That we'd be sealed in a compartment invulnerable to the realities of time and space. And that we'd be on a celebratory outing rather than playing out the last scene of our shared childhood.

Folding ourselves into the compartment, we faced each other on overstuffed cushions scented with rosewater, Binyamin's travel bag at his side. Spikes of sunlight tamed by the lace curtains intensified the excitement in his eyes before spilling into the gold-threaded interior. Then the bearers lifted the litter to sweep us southward through our quarter to the Canopic Way, westward to the Museum, northward on the Street of the Soma through the agora to the Caesareum, and finally along the harbor to his pier in the *Eunostos*, our western harbor.

"I really appreciate this send-off, Sis. I know you've been worried about me. But remember, I'm not studious like you. I could never spend the rest of my life bent over a ledger like Papa. So, I figure this is my best option. I could have enrolled in the *ludus* here, but I wouldn't get the same opportunities for training and competition that I'll have in Capua. Besides, I need to make the break for Papa's sake as well as my own. Can you imagine his reaction if I was training to be a gladiator right here in Alexandria?"

Some change in his expression, perhaps the slight parting of his lips or the lifting of his eyebrows, told me he was taking the moment to enjoy that fantasy.

"Binny, Binny, Binny, of course I've been worried about you." I didn't let on how worried, beginning with the voyage itself, not only the risk of a storm but the certainty of shipboard scoundrels waiting like vipers to feed on him. I only hoped he couldn't hear the apprehension in my voice.

"You're a part of me," I said, "the better part considering your grit, even as a child daring to confront Papa regardless of the consequences. And yes, I believe you could have a future in the arena. I just hope you're not doing this to atone for our mother's death. Papa may blame you, but her destiny was determined long before we were born."

"No, Sis, I really do love the games. You know I don't respect many things, but I do admire the Roman virtues gladiators represent: their discipline and dignity, their physical form and fearlessness, and their will to win. And Sergius says I got the gift."

Peeking through the curtains, watching the scenery slide by, I noticed we'd already turned onto the Canopic Way, its otherwise deserted concourse speckled with a few heat-drugged vendors hawking parasols and honey-sweetened water inside sharp-edged slivers of shade. Our bearers, their feet barely brushing the pavement, loped through the *Bruchium* Quarter, turning its colonnades and fountains, temples and monuments, sphinxes and statues into a radiant blur.

I was diverting Binyamin with a story when, distracted by a flock of twittering sand martins on wing to the beach, I peeked through the curtains to see that we'd already passed through the agora. Hearing the sea thunder and hiss against the rocks, I realized with a bile-swirling jolt that our jaunt was almost over, that the present was sliding toward the future all too quickly.

Then, thrusting his arm through the undulating curtain to signal the bearers to stop, he said in a flat voice, "I gotta go now, Sis."

Before his words could melt into the warm breeze, the bearers had lowered us to the curb. Grabbing his bag and bolting through the curtain, Binyamin began a run toward his pier. While I stayed listening to the rhythmic jingle of the clasps on his travel bag, I watched in the fading daylight his figure shrink to a minified silhouette before disappearing.

My brother ended up serving two five-year terms as a hired gladiator for the *ludus* in Capua and came home with his *rudis*, the wooden sword that symbolized the honorable discharge from his contract. But he also came home with the dream of owning the *ludus* in Alexandria, of turning it into the greatest in the empire. I swore never to reveal the entire story, but I can tell you now that to fulfill that dream, he'd committed heinous acts, making him too dangerous to trust at large. What's more, I was the only one to rein him in. Papa had tried and failed, and now it was up to me.

So, I told him: "Binyamin, you've done a terrible thing, actually many terrible things, all intentionally, all for your own gain. You're going to have to write all this down from the very beginning. And it better be the truth, none of your usual swagger and lies."

Of course, I was prepared for an onslaught of resistance.

He scratched his head, his brows creased as if in disbelief, and then it came. "What are you talking about? None of this was my fault." And with a scowl, he added, "Anyways, who are you to tell me what I have to do?"

His defiance was back, but it was milder than I expected. At least then.

"Besides, you know I can't write," he said, shifting in his seat as if he had hemorrhoids.

"Doesn't matter. Just write. Write as if you're talking to someone, as if you're explaining how it all happened, every detail."

"And if I don't?" he asked through gritted teeth.

"Then I'll have to write up my own account and deliver it to the magistrate personally."

So, he wrote it, all of it, but that was when I turned the tables on him. I kept my promise, as he knew I would. I didn't deliver his confession to the magistrate. But I told him that to earn the right to keep it confidential, he would have to join the *ludus* in Alexandria. Perhaps I'd hoped that by starting over and thereby doing penance for his crimes, he might even realize his dream of someday owning that *ludus*.

Of course, he fought me with anger, threats, and more—even guilt. So, when he insisted, for example, that with the new younger talent, he'd surely be killed in the arena, I countered by promising to buy back his body and provide a funeral for him, a magnificent memorial with an honorable burial and later an everlasting monument with his name and record as an outstanding gladiator.

"Ha! You expect me to believe that?" He wiped a string of spittle from his mouth with the back of his hand. "Just like Papa, you've opposed everything I ever wanted, but at least he did so openly."

And that was the last I'd heard either from or about Binyamin until Sergius came to visit me eight years ago, and of course today, when this unexpected undertow pulled him back into my life.

"Hey, Sis, stay with me, huh?"

Urged by the exasperation in his voice and a beam of full morning light, I blundered back to the Binyamin before me. "So, tell me, Binny, how in the name of holy Abraham did you manage to pull off this coming-back-to-life act?"

Warier than ever, casting sidelong glances for any sign of an eavesdropper, he took the other chair, moved it to face me, and sat down. Then, dropping his voice, he began the account I was eager to hear.

"I was severely injured in the arena." The harsh vowels of vulgar Latin had crept into his speech. "Some cocky new hire—Wouldn't you know it?—got lucky." He shrugged, his hands flapped open, palms up. "Of course, I don't remember everything, but Sergius was right there with the *libitinarii*." My brother leaned forward. As a competitive athlete, he'd learned to seldom blink, but he squinted with the same green eyes, hard as pebbles though smaller now, encircled by fat and a web of fine wrinkles. "You know who they are, right? The *libitinarii*? Those slaves who cart off the dead between bouts? Rather than just dump me in the *spoliarium*—"

"The *spoliarium*!" I gasped as my palm flew to my chest. "No!" His mention of that pit hurled me into that gruesome chamber under the arena, its indescribable stench, its dim patches of cold light, the squeals of its scrabbling rats, and the din of its slaves salvaging the armor and weaponry from the rows upon rows of corpses stacked clear to the ceiling!

"Yeah, Sis, the *spoliarium*! They say the slaves prepare the bodies for mass burial there. Ha!" He threw back his head and chilled me with a malignant bark of laughter. "You think they'd waste all that fresh meat? They cut us up and feed us to the beasts to whet their appetite for human flesh. But Sergius insisted they respect my right as a hired gladiator and take me to the *saniarium* first to see if I could be treated."

A wave of nausea spun through me, the porridge once more spurting up my gorge. Afraid I was going to faint again, I squeezed my eyes shut, swallowed the bitterness, and grabbed his arm for support.

His jaw set, his eyes narrowed in scarcely disguised impatience, he shook off my hand as if it were a pesky fly and resumed his story, but this time with a rising stridency. "I gotta tell you, Sergius was right there for me, has been since the beginning." And he added, his face sharpening, "If you don't remember him, you're a bigger ninny than I thought."

But no one could forget his ex-gladiator friend, our easy-to-recognize popular hero who'd taken refuge in Alexandria with Eppia, the senator's wife who'd given up her several hundred slaves, the villa in Rome, and her seaside estate in Antium to be with him. With a stump for a right arm, he had a dent in his head, a wart on the end of his nose, and an ichor trickling from his swollen eyes. The scuttlebutt had it that the senator was still searching for them.

Stories of Sergius still swirl about the agora that he'd been seen here or there, at the games or the theater. It was Sergius who brokered the sale of my brother to his first *ludus*, the one in Capua, the oldest in the empire and the school Spartacus made famous. And it was Sergius who'd sponsored Binyamin's trip there in exchange for a cut of both his signing fee and prize money.

Binyamin continued as if he'd been reading my thoughts. "Listen, I made a lot of money for that rascal. When he saw I was gonna recover, he snuck me out in a coffin. Can you believe that? And to a brothel! Ha! I swear he's got connections everywhere."

By now my brother, his face aflame, was flying high, convinced of his good fortune, no different after all from the rebellious brat who'd lure Zenon's voluptuous daughter into the pantry of her father's cookshop to relieve his lust.

"He hired the madame to look after me. That's when he and I cooked up this scheme, but knowing him, he could have had it in mind since the *saniarium*

I arched my eyebrows and pursed my lips, but he missed the sarcasm in my exaggerated pretense of surprise.

"What a guy! He told me I should stay dead to escape my debts." Binyamin shook his head, smiling with closed eyes as if dazzled by Sergius's sheer brilliance. "Oh, I know what you're thinking! From whoring—"

That was exactly what I was thinking.

And then, with his arrogance in full bloom, he retorted, "But you're wrong." Looking directly at me for the first time, he challenged me with his eyes. Then they slid away. "Not from whoring. As a world-class gladiator and a handsome one at that, I was showered in every city with the company of eager women, but they still expected expensive gifts to show off to their jealous friends."

His midsection had thickened, and his jowls had softened; he was after all thirty-four years old. Still etched with the scars of violence, his body reeked of power and exuded an unbridled sexual appetite. And he never showed deference to anyone, not by dropping his eyes or bending his knee.

"But I admit it," he conceded. "I'd also been running up debts from gambling, drinking, and whatnot. So, Sergius said I should stay dead. That way I'd break free of my contract with the *ludus* in Alexandria, which was getting on my nerves anyways. Could you believe it? I could get out from under all that and start fresh with a new identity he'd help me create."

Binyamin threw me an impish grin that turned to a smirk before it reached his eyes. "Look, Sis, I know you don't approve of my business dealings, but hey, I gotta live. And why pretend? I am who I am."

Oh, I certainly knew who he was. Still, once my shock faded, I hoped if only for a split second, that he'd grown up at least a little. But I just had to see that same swagger of insolence, that same boyhood smirk to remember his pranks, how he'd rush the mule carts as they clattered over the pavement. Athlete that he was, he'd vault over their tailgates and toss handfuls of fodder from the driver's scuttle into the street or worse yet, at the beggars, street philosophers, and soothsayers lining the boulevard.

Or he'd stay too long at the beach. Refusing to come out of the water, he'd tunnel under the waves, slicing through the foam, and challenge the breakers until our maid had to send for Papa's bearers to drag him out. And if that wasn't enough mischief, he'd cut geometry class or skip school entirely, not so much to savor his freedom as to spite Papa who'd refused to send him to a *collegium iuvenum* to study martial arts.

And all the while, I'd be his alibi, each of my lies contributing a strand to the entire web. "No, Papa, that couldn't have been Binyamin swiping fruit from the produce stand." In truth, his juggling act culminated in his tossing the vendor's pomegranates to a ring of adoring ragamuffins. Or "No, Papa, he couldn't have been filching candy from Apollon's *pantopoleion*," the general store with confections he could easily have paid for. "We were studying geometry in my suite all evening. Honest, Papa."

In exchange, Binyamin would teach me how to stand on my head, shinny up a tree, or take aim at a snake with his slingshot. And he'd coach me in boxing, showing me how to estimate my opponent's reach, maintain my footing on sand, and throw, duck, and even take a punch. Still, no matter how hard I tried, I could never outfox him, outrun him, or outmaneuver him, great athlete that he was. In fact, no one could. And so, he'd set his haughty eyes on the preeminent *ludus* at Capua.

My only question was why, after all these years, had he come to see me now?

* * *

Binyamin's always had a ready pretext to justify his schemes, so I was curious to hear his excuse for contacting me. So, I asked him: "Binny, you've been dead to me for eight years. Why tell me you're alive now?"

"Well, Sis, I gotta go back to what happened after I left the brothel. Sergius gave me a new identity and named me Aquila—not Binyamin and not my tag, Agrippa Fortitudo, but this brand new name. Still, he couldn't give me an entirely new life." My brother lifted his chin with pride, enjoying himself as he explained this piece of his life to me. "See, when I joined my first *ludus*, the one in Capua, and signed the sacred oath—you know, that's the contract for a volunteer, for a new hire like me—it bound me to the *ludus* for five years."

His voice took on a feverish intensity. "You count on winning, but if you lose, you're expected to redeem yourself by dying bravely, by offering your throat and directing your opponent's blade to that vital spot. The fans are used to slaughter; they've seen plenty of that. They wanna see the values that made Rome great: a love of glory, the desire to win, and a contempt for death."

"So, you gave away your liberty for a chance to die for the amusement of a Roman mob."

"No, Sis." Binyamin dismissed my comment with a shake of his head. "It's a matter of honor, something you wouldn't understand. By agreeing to suffer the worst punishment, even death, the gladiator earns the admiration of the crowd and fights with the rage of the truly desperate."

But I did understand. It was my poor brother's need for that admiration that drove him to the *ludus* in the first place. Instead of being proud of Binyamin's athletic accomplishments, Papa never missed an opportunity to rebuke him. Over and over, as blotches of anger spread from his neck to his hairline and he stirred the air with his forefinger, our father would say, "Binyamin, you've reached a new low. You're nothing but a reprobate, a disgrace to your mother's memory, and a stain on our family's name." Then like a madman, he'd retreat into a smoldering silence behind a slammed door.

My father's sister, my wise old Aunt Hannah, said it was because Papa blamed Binyamin for our mother's death. See, Binny and I are twins. When our mother felt life quicken inside her, my parents, to bless the birth, commissioned the writing of a *Sefer Torah*, a copy of the *Five Books of Moses*, for the Great Synagogue. My parents also arranged for a community celebration upon completion of the *Sefer Torah*. The thousand-year-old tradition of singing, praying, and dancing before the Holy Ark would take place on the first anniversary of our birth. But a day or two after we were born, the heat from my mother's heart began to escape, her pulse rate increased, and she began to vomit. As her strength ebbed, our father would stumble through the house carrying her from room to room, sometimes begging, other times commanding her fever to go away.

Her suffering ended when she died, but Papa's had only begun. Raw grief took hold of him. For weeks thereafter, he would tear at his clothes, and smothering himself in her soiled linen, filling his nostrils with her scent, he'd pound his body with his fists as if to pulverize the grief and expel it through his pores. And all the while, he'd be either gasping and heaving in a convulsive wave of sobs or whimpering for the loss of his beloved.

The physicians said our mother died of childbed fever, a condition Papa blamed on Binyamin's having been a breech baby. Binyamin blamed himself as well. So, instead of our parents dedicating the *Sefer Torah* to the birth of Binyamin and me, my father ended up dedicating it to the memory of our mother. And Binny grew more and more reckless as if to tempt retribution from the three white-robed Fates who'd marked him a killer.

I'd forget we were twins because we were so different. He was the ginger-curled, high-spirited boy who, scorning our Jewish customs, morphed into the profligate Roman, a monstrous caricature of his former self, indifferent to the suffering of others. Convinced of his own superiority, he believed he was the center of the universe and could make it yield to his wishes.

On the other hand, I was the obedient little girl, a Jewess committed to our way of life despite our father's tirades. As harsh as he was to Binyamin, with me, his anger would disappear as quickly as a stone thrown into a pond. I was the favored child with chestnut braids and darkly fringed eyes who grew to resemble the tall, graceful woman he'd loved and lost.

"Hey, Sis, you slipping away on me again?" I could smell his annoyance in the souring of his breath.

I signaled for him to continue his drone by rolling my hand in impatient circles, but by then, with the late morning heat pouring in from the peristyle, I only pretended to be attentive with an occasional nod. Still, I managed to remember the substance of his account despite the porridge once again snaking up into the back of my throat.

"Anyways, when you sign the contract, you're branded on the face and legs as property of the *ludus*. Okay," he said, his voice croaking now. "I had the new name Aquila, but without the fame of my past life, only its scars and tattoos, the only jobs I could get were temporary. So, I worked now and then as a shitty bodyguard, posts Sergius would get for me for a finder's fee, of course. Like I said, I made a lot of money for that rich bastard.

"Wait! Didn't I tell you that already? I can't remember shit," he said, dropping his head and rubbing his temples with the heel of his hands. "Sergius made up a story for me—Oh, you'll love this one, a real sob story—that I'd been orphaned and survived on the streets by my wits— Ha! I really liked that part—on Rome's *Alta Semita* as a petty thief and pickpocket. 'One day,' Sergius said, 'you tried to pick the pocket of a guy named Cyrus who let's say happened to be the *lanista* at the *ludus* in Pergamon. When this dickhead supposedly called for a soldier to arrest you, he was so impressed with your nerve and the way you fought that he recruited you right then and there for his *ludus*.' A stupid-ass story, I know, but I could stick to it 'cause when I'd traveled with the troupe of gladiators from Capua, I got a taste of those piss-poor neighborhoods in Rome, and I must have fought in Pergamon a million times. Anyways, at least five or six I can remember."

* * *

I was getting so tired of my brother's bluster that I chewed the inside of my cheek to stay alert until even that didn't work. My mind wandered to my appointment at noon with Professor Jason, the leper-white, thin-lipped physician at the medical school who investigates the deaths that baffle the magistrates. His colleagues may mock him for his unorthodox conclusions, but when I was working on the deaths of those two cousins dying from the same familial ill—

Binyamin jolted my thoughts as he smacked his fist on the arm of his chair. "Now here comes the good part."

So, I was swept back into listening, this time hoping for something interesting.

"This hunchbacked street philosopher was preaching the end of slavery. What an asshole! Anyways, he caused this traffic jam. Wheels clattered to a stop, whips cracked, men shouted and cursed. So, there I was standing under the portico of *The Hestia*, my favorite brothel near the *Circus Maximus*, waiting for a brawl to break out. It always does with those guys, you know? That's when I like to knock out a few teeth just to show those sissies how to fight.

"But before any of them even threw a punch, my eyes slid down the block to what sounded like a dying animal, except it was this impossibly skinny, bird-shouldered boy in a fancy litter being beaten by a pair of thugs. The bigger one, like a Cyclops with pillars for legs and battering rams for arms, held the kid down while the dwarf—I swear to Zeus, he looked just like Caligula with those ears sticking out from his triangular face. Anyways, the dwarf kept pulling at the kid's neck, trying to steal what must have been the father's torc—"

"That helpless boy! Why was he left alone in the street?" The grievance in my voice surprised me, not loud but penetrating.

"No kidding. The bearers were supposed to have been guarding him, but with the bottleneck—hey, nothing was getting through—they must have figured the kid would be safe for a while. So, they slipped away to listen. Except once they did that, nobody—not just the riffraff but the wagons, oxcarts, drays—hey, you name it—like I said, nobody would give even an inch when they tried to tear back to the kid."

"So, what did the thugs want— "

"Well, like I was saying, the kid had on a torc, this rigid neck ring made of strands of gold twisted together. It must have been awarded to the father for his rank as a legionnaire. But this one had a hook and ring closure that was too tight for the dwarf to open. So, in disgust, the Cyclops threw the kid into—"

My palm flew to my chest again while Binyamin sat back, nodding with an evil grin.

"—the Tiber. Itching for action, that was all I needed to see. Now you know I can slice through water, right? So, I kicked through the crowd—boy, you should have seen them jump—Ha!—And then I dove off the nearest bridge and pulled him out of the water like a fish on a hook. Turns out he was crippled besides."

"But he was okay?"

"Slow down, Sis. I'm not there yet. Never mind the kid. Wanna know what happened to the bearers? The boy's father could have had them crucified, but instead he had them thrown to the lions. Nothing like something quick and grisly to please the crowd." Binyamin threw his head back and broke out in peals of malicious laughter as he rocked back and forth in his chair.

That laugh was only too familiar to me.

"Don't you get it, Sis? They stopped to listen to some preacher about the end of slavery, and theirs ended all right, just like that." Binyamin snapped his fingers.

I stared so hard that I saw two cruel, hawklike faces instead of one.

"Don't you think that's funny?" His cold eyes crawled all over my face, waiting for a response. "Oh, Neptune's balls! You're the same sourpuss you always were. Don't think I'll ever forget that it was you who made me join that piss-poor excuse for a *ludus* in Alexandria. And

I know why, too. With me dead, you could control the family business all by yours—"

"No, Binn—"

"Well, let me tell you, I'm not gonna play nanny to a spoiled brat for the rest of my life either. Someday I'm gonna own that dinky *ludus*. You'll see! I'll turn it into the greatest spectacle in the empire, the envy of every *lanista*, and make a fortune besides."

Flecks of spittle formed at the corners of his mouth. He wiped them away with the back of his hand.

"The least you could do is say how proud you are of me. The boy's grateful mother persuaded her husband to give me a handsome reward and a permanent place in the family protecting their son. But no, you think I'm just good for whoring, drinking, gambling, and, oh yeah, killing. Well, for your information, I've been with this family several years now. When the father retired three years ago, he moved the household to his estate on Lake Mareotis, just south of the city walls. Not me, of course. I wouldn't be a resident nursemaid to any jerk, even a rich one—*especially* a rich one—living out in the sticks in some outbuilding like a slave. No, thanks. I prefer my own haunts. Anyways, that's why I came back to Alexandria, reluctantly I might add, for the job with that legionnaire. But I figured I'd better let you know so you stay out of my way."

With that, he unfolded all six feet of his height, spat a medallion of greasy phlegm at my feet, and knocking over a planter of yellow field marigolds, stalked out through the peristyle.

How quickly we'd resumed our childhood antagonisms.

* * *

Even in the molten midday heat, the old soldierly professor strode into my study with the sinuous grace of a big cat and the energy of a young man.

"Thank you for seeing me, Miss bat Isaac, especially on such short notice." Although he still spoke in the precisely articulated diction of a scholar, instead of his usual stentorian voice, deep enough to boom across a lecture hall, his tone was as thin and dry as a sheet of papyrus.

Once he'd taken a seat across from my desk and arranged his limbs, I noticed he'd grown thinner than when I last saw him two years ago. And looking more closely, I saw that his hair was a shade whiter, and the creases scouring his brow were deeper. But if I squinted, I could see the man as he was when we last worked together to investigate the death of a coquettish Roman matron. Still, I was puzzled. Why would such a learned man be consulting me and with a quaver in his voice besides? So, I dispensed with the usual pleasantries and waited for him to begin.

"The wife of an old friend of mine has been kidnapped, and I'm helpless to assist. No doubt they've been singled out because of his family's wealth. She's been gone only a day, but her husband has already gotten a ransom demand in which the swine threatens to kill her unless an enormous sum is paid."

The professor's disquiet filled me with a chilling curiosity. "First, let me express my regret that such a wicked event should have happened, especially to a friend of yours, and my hope that we can bring her home safely." I tried to sound more confident than I felt. "What's more, keep in mind that criminals leave useful information behind in the form of clues."

Professor Jason dipped into the leather purse secured to his belt and withdrew a drawstring pouch. "This sealed pouch came to my friend yesterday. It contained this scrap of papyrus and a ring, which he says his wife wore all the time." He spread out the items on my desktop. "My friend had given her this ring shortly after their move to Alexandria. That's her portrait in mosaics set in malachite."

I had to pick up that ring. I not only recognized the jeweler's craftsmanship but the pouch as well. My husband delivers all his handiwork in bluish-purple, silk pouches like that.

Then I reached for the ransom note. If Alexander's horse had materialized in my peristyle, I couldn't have been more surprised. That scrap of papyrus was smooth enough to have been torn from the finest sheet. As a little girl visiting one of the many papyrus factories along Lake Mareotis, I'd watch how the workers used needles to split the plant stems into strips—the longer and thinner the better. But the strips from the center of the stem made the smoothest—and most expensive— sheets. So, I found the high quality of the papyrus perplexing.

Next I read the note. The first half was written in an elegant hand, ornate with rounded letters and flourishes the husband recognized as his wife's. In it she pled for her husband to meet the kidnappers' demand so she could return to his loving arms. The rest was scrawled in faint, barely legible, knock-kneed letters. Still the message was clear: The kidnappers threatened to torture her with hot coals every day until the ransom was paid. Moreover, they vowed to burn her alive if the authorities were contacted or the ransom was not deposited in a particular account at the Bank of Gabinius by the calends.

That gives us only two days!

"Who is your old friend?"

The professor answered after a sigh and a small shake of his great head. "I wish I could tell you, but I can't, not without his permission. Foolish I know, but he's so afraid of the kidnappers that if they find out he's launched an investigation, they'll just kill his wife and run."

And he certainly doesn't want someone like me involved, not with my official connection to the magistrates. He just wanted some advice. I argued to the contrary, urging him to give me permission to reveal his name or at least contact the authorities himself, but there was no changing his mind.

A heavy frown creased his face, but then the professor resumed his usual academic countenance. "So, I thought I'd come to you. I know you're discreet and have handled cases like this before."

The question still burned my tongue, but chasing away any attempt to speculate on his friend's identify, I switched to another line of inquiry: "Have there been any strange absences from his household?"

"What an idiot I am!" he said, slapping his forehead with an open palm. "I should have asked him that!"

"Well, can you at least tell me how the ransom demand was delivered?"

"*Hmm.*" The professor crossed and recrossed his legs. "A courier-for-hire brought it to my friend's doorkeeper, who barely got a glimpse of the fellow through the grid over the peephole. When asked, the doorkeeper didn't think he'd recognize the bearer again. He said, 'The fellow could be any of a hundred Egyptian couriers in the city. Besides, they all look alike.'"

"I'll begin my investigation with the delivery of the ransom demand," I said, "and contact you with any information I can garner."

We stood simultaneously. As I walked him through the atrium to show him out, I felt as if I were entering a burning building, its pillars of smoke blinding my eyes as they rose to merge with the sky.

Chapter Three: Phoebe

"Miriam, it's me, Phoebe," I said as I barged into the atrium and circling around the *impluvium*, the shallow rainwater basin that serves to cool the atrium, charged into her study. "I got here as fast as I could."

Miriam was standing in front of her ebony desk, gazing with troubled eyes on a corner of the ceiling as though trying to decipher some code written there. What she saw, I have no idea, but her alabaster skin and the lines and planes of her face reminded me of a delicately carved cameo. When she sensed my presence, her eyes found their way to my face.

My nerves had been tingling since her bearer, Orestes—the one I think of as wearing the winged hat and shoes of Mercury—knocked on my door. He told me there was no time to lose if I wanted to work with Miriam on a kidnapping. But the best light of the day had already faded by the time my bearers carried me from my townhouse near the north end of the Street of the Soma, through the crushing traffic of the Canopic Way, to Miriam's home in the Jewish Quarter. As we pressed through the throng of gawkers and hawkers, the pungent smells of mules and camels, and the geysers of dust behind them, my ears were assaulted by the mournful howl of a stray dog, the clamor of craftsmen in their workshops, and the harangue of soothsayers promising a miracle for a price.

I was the Greek foundling Mother Isis saved and Miriam's mother fostered. The story is that she found me wrapped in a soiled blanket in the *Bruchium* Quarter when hardly more than a day old. The long-established practice of my people abandoning their infant daughters had resurfaced in Egypt as a symptom of our hardship under the Roman occupation. Miriam's mother carried me home, hired a wet nurse for my first three years, and then undertook to rear me as a domestic slave. Later, when I was ten, Miriam's father invited me to take lessons with his five-year-old daughter. Since then she and I have become the best of friends. Only when I married Bion, a freedman who used his quitclaim to buy a *bibliopōleion*, the grandest bookstore in the city, did I ask for my freedom so our children would be free.

One thing about Miriam, she's always late. So, I try to emphasize my promptness, hoping she'll change. So far, no luck. In fact, in this case when I told her how fast I'd come, I not only didn't impress her, but she was actually cross with me.

"Oh, there you are!" she said, eyeing me with benevolent exasperation. "I'd all but given up on you!"

"Miriam, that's not fair!" Couldn't she hear that my breathing was labored? To my own ears, I sounded like a bellows. "I'd just gotten back from working in the soup kitchen when Orestes told me to come right away. By the way, we'll never have enough soup if the Romans keep increasing the poll tax and—"

"Pheeb, I have a mission I can entrust only to—"

"I know. I know. I'm your full-fledged partner now since we solved my neighbor's—"

"No, Pheeb," Miriam said, wagging her finger back and forth. "Not we. *You.* You did it with your courage and determination."

And a little help from Isis, whose power transcends that of all other deities. "But I didn't finish telling you about my morning."

Another thing about Miriam, she gets impatient with me. I can tell when she tucks her upper lip inside her lower lip, but this time she also bobbed her foot up and down. She also complains that I embroider events with too many ghoulish details, sensational opinions, and theatrical exaggerations, but my findings, she says, are nevertheless sound. And so, she recently promoted me from being her intrepid scout to not just her permanent number one deputy but her full-fledged partner and gave me a three-layered, sardonyx cameo of Isis to mark the occasion.

"Pheeb, about that mission. I need to tell—"

"Well, what do you think I've been waiting for?" That's what I meant about Miriam. She gets impatient with me when it should really be the other way around. I know it's all envy, untouched by bitterness, of course, so I excuse it.

I dropped my bulk into one of the *curule* chairs, and sitting opposite me, she clapped her hands for some refreshments. Soon enough, Calisto brought us a silver tray with a krater of wine and crystal goblets. Miriam ladled the wine into our goblets, and then as soon as she nodded, Calisto bowed and melted away without even a rustle of her tunic or the whisper of her slippered feet on the mosaic floor.

I reached for the goblet like a desert nomad, my bosom casting a shelf-like shadow over the tablecloth. Curling my hand around the stem, I downed it all and smacked my lips. "A perfect blend with the pomegranate juice, Miriam. Could I have a little more? Please? Just a splash."

She responded with the twitch of a smile and refilled my goblet.

Miriam pinched the stem of her goblet between her thumb and forefinger, and splaying out her other fingers, took a dainty sip. Tapping her mouth with her napkin, she leaned forward and with an urgency in her voice, told me about Professor Jason's visit.

Despite the steady pulse of the late afternoon heat, I shivered like a frightened horse upon hearing the words "kidnap," "ransom," and "kill."

She ended by saying, "So, while I work on finishing these accounts before the *nones*, I want you to find that courier and bring him here."

That was when my fascination turned to a bowel-wrenching dread. "But—but like the doorkeeper said," I stammered, "the courier could be any Egyptian, which means he likely lives in the *Rhakotis* Quarter."

Miriam's father had once characterized the *Rhakotis* Quarter, our third residential district, as having the dreariest buildings, dustiest yards, grimmest alleys, foulest gutters, vilest graffiti, hungriest mosquitoes, scrawniest cats, filthiest children, saddest drunks, and the oldest whores. In fact, it was that two-mile-wide tongue of limestone between the Mediterranean Sea and Lake Mareotis—an old fishing village, pirates' nest, and Egyptian outpost—that Alexander the Great recognized as having the potential to become our great city.

But today, the *Rhakotis* Quarter, where most of the Egyptians still live, is blighted by poverty, pestilence, and violence. And no one seems to care who's beaten or murdered in the streets and then dumped into that foul canal to soak, bloat, float, and putrefy in the next day's baking sun.

"Yes, Phoebe, he likely lives in the *Rhakotis* Quarter, and that's why I need your courage and determination for the job. What's more, I'll send Orestes to protect you."

Miriam was going to lend me her very best. As a young investment banker, her father had bought Orestes and Solon to transport him through the city in style. Despite the passing years, both bearers have remained strong, top-heavy men with huge, veiny hands and thick, ropy necks. But of the two, Orestes is the plucky one who sparkles with energy, whereas Solon is the sleepy-eyed dreamer who moves as if he's wading through a thick liquid.

I felt as if I'd swallowed poison and was waiting to die right on the spot, but I was committed. So, I took one more greedy gulp of wine and wondered how my promotion to full-fledged partner had changed anything in my business with Miriam.

* * *

My bearers swept Orestes and me westward along the Canopic Way as the final shreds of daylight painted the colonnades, sphinxes, temples, and monuments with a smear of color. But as the chill of the night replaced the heat of the day, my soul enjoyed none of that sweetness, not the balmy breezes through the cypress trees, the glow of torches twinkling through the foliage, nor the tuneless twitter of birds returning to roost. Instead, Isis helped me focus on a plan to find the one courier in this vast city who'd brought the ransom note to Professor Jason's friend. I started my inquiry with the couriers in front of the Palace of Justice as they waited to make their last runs of the day.

Bats were circling into the dusk as we stepped out of the litter. Even with Orestes standing behind me, my whole body quaked as if I were possessed. But with a plea to Isis, I took hold of my courage and approached the crowd of walnut-colored men. Squatting in the street, their voices tumbling over each other, I could grasp only scraps of their conversations. Most I knew to ignore.

At last, with an imperious wave, I managed to get enough of their attention to hurl out a few words: "…Delivery yesterday to Lake…?"

"What's it to you, lady?" The man, his face marked by dark spidery veins, spoke in a clumsy Greek but with the sharply clipped consonants of his Egyptian patois.

Sounding like the growl of a feral dog closing in on its prey, a mix of their voices rolled up to support this challenger among them.

I waited, taking an exasperated sigh but to no avail.

"Did I leave it under your bed?" That question was spit-sprayed from the toothless mouth in front of me while a thread of saliva clung to his lower lip.

A round of guffaws rose up like the sea in a storm.

I waved my arm again but this time with a shiny *denarius* in my hand, likely their entire earnings for a single day.

An edgy silence expanded like a dark gas. Even the breeze and birds quieted. The only noises were an occasional cough and the sputter of a single ember as it broke off a nearby torch.

I waited for the silence to harden before speaking again. "Did anyone here deliver a pouch to Lake Mareotis a couple of days ago?"

A rumble of pleas scraped my ears like a razor while a dozen or so men elbowed toward me. So, I just shook my head and raised my palms. But then a gangly, knob-limbed fellow with hollow cheeks came forward, his face tilting up as he shouted to me.

"Gimme, gimme." He stretched out an arm as thin as a stick to reach for the *denarius*. "Was that knucklehead, Abasi!" Despite missing two fingers, he deftly snatched the coin. "Bragging in The Lizard's Tail about that tip from the sender, not that he didn't crab about having to go outside them city walls and back with no return fare. 'Got nothing from that rat-faced doorkeeper.' That's what he done said, 'Got nothing. Doorkeeper just stood there like a dumb statue.'"

I lifted my eyes for some reassurance from Isis and then turned my gaze for a signal from Orestes. When he jerked his head in the direction of the *Rhakotis* Quarter, I knew we'd be going to The Lizard's Tail that very night. But before we boarded my litter, he raised his forefinger to me. "The yards of silk and the bronze fittings on your litter won't protect you from the thieves and murderers who prey in the darkness. Let me tuck your purse under my belt in case we encounter bandits along the way."

As he hid the purse, I noticed the hilt of a dagger protruding from the sheath on his belt.

* * *

We rode westward into the dusty smell of the wind, the inky shadows shifting and sliding in the trembling cones of light from the torches lining the Canopic Way. Otherwise, all colors and landmarks disappeared. Once we entered the *Rhakotis* Quarter, crossed over that slime-coated canal, and followed it northward, the gloom was relieved by only the funnel of light trembling in my lead bearer's hand.

Neither Orestes nor I spoke. Instead, we sat as still as stones while both thrill and dread consumed me. Only the sounds of the night filled the litter: the thrum of wings, the chirr of insects, the squeals of rats, the moan of the sea, and the wheeze of the wind. Checking our wake, I saw my rear bearer lower his head and hunch his shoulders as he leaned into the gusts that raised whorls of grit, swayed the trees, and tore at the layers of gauze draping my litter.

And then for a time, everything went quiet. Unnaturally so, like after a door slams. Even the wind ceased. The silence was so thick it was as if my bearers had to paddle through it.

Until I heard a noise, dry and brittle, probably not so loud as it seemed.

Orestes and I exchanged a look.

He took a deep intake of breath.

Firm footfalls on the cobbles, faint at first but drawing nearer and louder.

Then, from those footfalls, a beam of light shot through the darkness.

Orestes's hand dropped to his belt.

As quick as a viper, one of the arms behind that light grabbed my lead bearer's lantern and threw it to the pavement. As soon as I heard the hollow clatter, the lantern flared, fizzled, and died.

Orestes sprang to life, leaped out of the litter, his dagger unsheathed, and shouted, "Stop!" That single word, like a rising howl, throbbed with menace. An instant later, one of Orestes's hands cupped the back of viper-arm's head while his other hand pressed the tip of his dagger against the thug's throat.

"What do you want, shiteater?" Orestes bellowed. "Tell me quick. Your life depends on it."

A moment later, Isis was yanking me out of the litter and to my dismay, pointing her staff at the outlaw's lantern. Rushing him, I grabbed it and framed him in its feverish brightness.

It was as if I were looking at a savage-faced tree rather than a human being. His nutmeg skin, weathered like the bark of a sun-scalded olive tree, was seamed with splits and grooves while his body, cloaked in black, merged with the night.

But the Tree didn't answer. Instead, he drove an elbow into Orestes's chin.

After that, everything happened at once.

Orestes lurched backward, arms pinwheeling, his dagger clanging to the pavement. But thanks to Isis, he regained his balance to punch his opponent at the beltline, his shoulders behind the storm of blows.

The Tree then caught Orestes with a double jab to the nose and a roundhouse swing that clipped the side of his head, blasted the air out of him, and sent him sprawling. But getting his breath back, he was able to scoop up his dagger from the cobbles. Then, standing swiftly, facing his attacker, and bending his right knee, he lunged forward, wielding the blade. I can still hear its metallic ring as he swept it across the Tree's cheekbone.

Ribbons of blood trickled through the grooves in the Tree's face, making it look more than ever as if it were carved from bark. At the same time, his mouth twisting in agony, a crimson rain pooled onto the cobbles.

As the Tree assessed the wound with his fingertips, Orestes crashed into him, burned him with a flurry of sledgehammer fists, and watched him crumple to the pavement.

He didn't move.

With the throb of military boots approaching, I thrust our newly acquired lantern into my lead bearer's hand. Then Orestes and I scrambled into the litter. My bearers paused only long enough to exchange a silent signal before taking their positions to speed us through a rutted, rubble-strewn alley smelling of rotgut, garbage, and cat piss. And so, we were off again, continuing toward the district lining the *Eunostos*.

* * *

With only a foam of stars to relieve the shrillness of the moonless sky, I inched close to Orestes as if his body could shield me from the dramas of the night. Along the way, we passed a lone drunk slumped against a tree. I figured he was a sailor or roustabout who'd emptied his purse shooting dice and stopped for a drink or two to soften the blow. Later we heard the screech and rumble of a mule-drawn cart, probably a produce vendor making his early-morning deliveries to the inns, saloons, and cookshops near the docks. Otherwise, the street was deserted. I felt threatened just the same.

How slowly the time passed, as if invisible hands were stretching each treacherous minute. Knowing that each bump, twist, and turn through the narrow, dung-tufted warrens was bringing us closer to our destination, I kept busy gnawing on my cuticles and spitting out the skin so that by the time we reached the grimmest back streets, I could taste the blood on my lips.

Those streets with their five- and six-story flat-faced, tumbledown tenements were jammed together like spectators at the games. The odors of poverty and neglect—a combination of animal droppings, stale urine, and sluggish gutters clogged with decaying leaves—hung over their weed-strewn yards to sting my nose. But that was how I knew we were close to The Lizard's Tail.

Sure enough, the darkness was soon shattered by the coarse glare and tawdry brilliance of the drinking dens, gaming parlors, brothels, and the sleazy inns like The Pegasus that cater to sailors, carters, and slaves. I was familiar with that inn, of course, because Professor Jason and I had investigated the suspicious death of a retired gladiator there, but Miriam had also worked a case there, the brutal murder of her father's former scribe, who'd been bludgeoned to death in his room. And even before that, Binyamin had stayed there to await his ship's departure for Rome's port of Ostia before trekking along the Appian Way to his *ludus* in Capua.

The jolt of the litter as the bearers lowered us into a dank, rock-strewn alley brought me back to the night's mission. "We're here," I said to Orestes, pointing to a bar of light across the street-level entrance to a hovel flanked by two others, a wine shop and a souvenir store, where they sell those bronze statuettes that tourists buy of the Pharos Lighthouse and the Serapeum. All three were crouched together as if to brace themselves against the briny gusts of wind. The paint on the door to The Lizard's Tail was peeling like dead skin, exposing patches of the silvery wood beneath, but enough of a lizard's tail remained on the signboard to assure me that my bearers had found the right place.

"You first," I said to Orestes, "and before settling down with something for yourself, be sure to bring some wine, a few hunks of bread and cheese, and anything else you can carry out to the bearers. Then I'll go in. I want to speak with the courier, this Abasi, or at least find out about him. I think he'll speak more freely if he thinks I'm alone."

Orestes nodded, and as the door groaned open, he disappeared in a flash of lamplight, a burst of manly noise, and a complex of sour smells that escaped through the open door. I waited in the alley with the bearers, who after eating, would likely take turns resting in the litter until we were ready to leave. Unless of course, there was trouble. But as the morning light began to gather in the east and wash away the darkness in the west, the taste of last night's sinister stew began to fade.

Orestes came out with an amphora of wine and foods wrapped in linen napkins. In addition to the bread and cheese, he brought some figs, nuts, and warm honey cakes. Then once he was back in the saloon, Isis tapped me on the shoulder, her signal that now it was my turn. Despite the fatigue that had engulfed me in the litter, I felt the spring of excitement as I took a deep breath and slapped the dust off the skirt of my *stola*.

* * *

The Lizard's Tail was clearly the favorite watering hole for the coarser elements of the neighborhood. Even in those wee hours, the boisterous voices of sweaty dockworkers buzzed around me like a swarm of gnats. They punctuated their clipped consonants and ribald comments with thumps on the table that rattled the cutlery and crockery.

The air from the kitchen carried the stink of fried grease, rotten fish, and boiled cabbage. But as my *calcei* waded through the sawdust into the belly of the saloon, into its heavy-beamed dark ceiling, rows of wall-mounted oil lamps, and shelves of dusty bottles, my nose caught whiffs as well of slimy vegetables, mice droppings, and spewed *henket*, a cheap Egyptian beer.

The interior was long and narrow with some thirty men—Orestes among them—sitting on rough wooden benches along two trestle tables that end-to-end spanned the length of the room. While they ate, drank, laughed, cursed, and quarreled, the stout peg-legged proprietor and his jolly red-faced wife passed steaming plates, drinks, and coins back and forth up and down the rows.

For the moment, I was nearly overwhelmed by the sounds whirling around me, but Isis nudged me to approach the wife. "A...Abasi," I stammered.

"What?" she thundered over the commotion.

"Abasi. I want to speak to Abasi."

"Abasi?" she boomed again, this time her eyes narrowing and her brow puckering as if my request was preposterous.

A stunned silence fell on the room like a blanket. I heard only the sputter of a single candle. The men gaped at each other before erupting in a chorus of guffaws. At the same time, some pointed a knife, spoon, or forefinger—whatever was handy—at a concave-chested fellow, thin as a starving cat, with mud-encrusted fingernails and a head as bald as an onion. Others doubled over, pounded each other's back, or held their bellies as whoops of lighthearted laughter swept through the saloon. Even the cook peeped out from the kitchen, his fat cheeks blotched and jiggling, to contribute to the mirth. The hilarity would wane and then bubble up again until everyone was either wiping his eyes, blowing his nose, or running to the latrine.

I tugged at a corner of Mrs. Jolly's apron and pulled her aside with a question in my eyes.

She explained. "Men been teasing Abasi, coaxing him to get married. But he's so shy, afraid to even approach a woman. When you asked for him, they thought a fancy lady like you was gonna be his wife."

"I'm so sorry. I didn't mean to embarrass—"

"Nah," she said, waving her hand to brush away my apology. "They always making a fuss over him, only one of them still single."

"Please ask him to step into the alley. I'm here to make him a business offer."

By then, Orestes had moved toward the back, near the alley exit. Having grabbed a candle from the end of the table, he was crouching under the cobwebbed eaves as if studying the ships' departure schedules mounted on the rear wall. Just as I was about to cross the threshold into the alley, a hiss and display of small teeth warned me that I was sharing the doorway with the saloon's eponymous, spiny-tailed lizard about to swing its spiked tail at my bare ankles. Yikes! I was out of there in one breathless moment, accompanied by another wave of guffaws directed at either me or the lizard.

Making my way toward the litter, the sun high enough now to reach into the alley, I welcomed the warmth of the new day, the sight of ships looming out of the shadows, the wind whistling in their rigging, and one with a tall mast clinging like a toy to the horizon. Soon enough, Mrs. Jolly was pushing her reluctant customer out the back door, Orestes right behind them. Abasi swallowed the last of his supper and sucked his snaggled teeth to clear the food caught between them. Then, looking back more than once at Mrs. Jolly standing at the open door, he formed a visor with his hand against an arrow of sunlight and peered into the alley, his wary eyes flitting from one object to another until they settled on me with the raw look of a frightened animal.

"I'm sorry to interrupt your meal, Abasi. I'm here about a reward you might qualify for, but first I need to know whether you made a delivery to an estate on Lake Mareotis the day before yesterday."

He shook his head as he shrugged. "No, lady—"

I raised my palm to silence him. "I assure you, you're not in any kind of trouble."

"What if I did?"

"Well, can you describe what you brought?"

"What d'ya wanna know?"

Perhaps I was getting somewhere. "What did it look like?"

"Who ya gonna tell?"

"My friend sent me. She wants to find out who hired you. But first we want to make sure you were the one who delivered it. That's why I need you to describe it."

"Don't remember."

"Oh, that's too bad. She's willing to pay a lot of money for that information."

He closed his eyes, shook his head, and bit his lower lip.

"A lot of money," I repeated.

"Maybe it was somethin' like a darkish blue pouch with a drawstrin'. Smooth too."

"Anything else?"

"Yeah. I go outside the city walls and got nothin' from that rat-faced doorkeeper."

"I think you're the courier my friend is looking for. I would like you to come with me now to my friend's house. She'll ask you a few more questions and then give you the reward."

He ground the heels of his hands into his eyes as if trying to comprehend his good fortune and then joined Orestes and me in the litter, where I watched the morning sun varnish the buildings while Isis rocked me to sleep.

Chapter Four: Miriam

I never expected Phoebe to find the courier in less than a day. But sure enough, late the next morning, after putting him up in the outbuilding where my bearers lodge, Orestes brought me a scraggly-looking man, bald as a plucked turkey and with a mouth of crooked oversized teeth. My intrepid bearer, his arm threaded around the courier's shoulder, announced "Abasi" with some weight and encouraged him with a pat on the arm to enter through the great mahogany doors of my study.

With a look back at Orestes, who threw him a reassuring nod, the courier inched forward. I coaxed him in with an outstretched arm and waved him toward the chair across from my desk. He sat hunched forward, his profile half turned toward me, but he kept his eyes down, his sharp chin tucked against his concave chest.

"Thank you for coming. If you're the courier who delivered a pouch three days ago to an estate on Lake Mareotis, I want to give you a reward. Was that you?"

When he lifted his chin and bobbed his head slowly, I knew he understood my question.

"Who gave you the pouch?"

"Street urchin," he said with a shrug. "Dark. Ragged. Barefoot."

"How did he find you?"

"Comin' out of The Lizard's Tail. Kid come up to me with this pouch.

Gimme lot of money."

That certainly didn't sound like something the kidnapper would do, hand over money to some street urchin. He'd know that the kid would take the money, perhaps the ring as well, and throw the rest of the pouch into the canal.

"Look Abasi, I know you deserve the reward, but I can't give it to you unless you tell me the truth." I reached into the basket near the corner of my desk for a *denarius*, lay the coin on my palm, and extended my hand to him. "You delivered the pouch as you were told, so the man who gave it to you has no reason to hurt you. Just tell me what he looked like."

"Big. Scars and tattoos."

"Was anyone else around?"

He cocked his head. "Lots. Dockworkers, sailors headin' for the midday meal."

"What else can you tell me about the pouch?"

"Sealed."

"Did the seal bear any identifying information?"

He shook his head.

"And where did you deliver it?"

"Estate on the lake, fountains, and these big bronze doors."

"Can you tell me anything else?"

"Tight-assed doorkeeper." Abasi shook his head, his upper lip raised in disgust.

And so, I rewarded Abasi with the *denarius*, though his information hardly seemed worth even that. After walking him to the atrium for Calisto to show him out, I made my way back to my desk, massaging my temples, any hope of a quick solution dripping away like wax on a melting candle.

* * *

I wanted to consult with my husband, Judah. Based on his taste, the craftsmanship of the ring, and the design of the pouch, I knew they were his creations. I just needed to find out more about this client of his and the household. Who could have known its routines well enough to execute a kidnapping? So, I summoned Orestes and Solon to take me to Judah's shop in the agora.

Perfect timing. By the time they dropped me off at the gate, the agora was, as expected, deserted in the midafternoon drowse. The shops were empty, shuttered against the scorching heat, while the pitiless sun roasted the soles of my *calcei*, set the treetops ablaze, and hammered down on the tents and barrows, wagons and moneychangers' tables. I heard only an idler's phlegmy snores bubbling out from a polygon of shade and the whine of a mangy dog that glowered but did nothing else to challenge me.

Lulled by the afternoon heat, my mind took me back almost twenty years to the calends following my sixteenth birthday. Until then, love had been an abstraction to me, the substance of myths and legends. But that was the day Papa, at long last reconciled to Binyamin's contempt for the investment business, asked me to collect the payments from his mortgagors in the agora. And so that was the day I met Judah, the jeweler with the high-bridged nose and rugged cleft chin, broad shoulders and chiseled muscles, glossy black curls and thickly lashed, luminous green eyes.

When I'd entered Judah's shop, he raised his lids to look at me and squared his shoulders with a slow, deep, almost guttural intake of breath. With his even slower exhale, I felt a flutter in my belly that was both pleasure and pain. Later, as I was leaving, he leaned toward me, close enough for our air to mingle and for his palm to brush against mine when he handed me his payment. That sensation of his nearness ignited my embryonic fantasies of love and unleashed a longing that was both mystical and earthly, passionate and tender, shy and eager.

But, apart from collecting his mortgage payments, Papa wanted me to have nothing to do with Judah. Generations ago, our family had purchased Roman citizenship, a privilege that's hereditary only when both parents are citizens. Roman citizenship guarantees redress in the Roman courts as well as immunity from the most onerous taxes and services. But Judah was the illegitimate son of an orphaned woman. Not only was he reared without the respectability of a father's name, but without citizenship, he had no protection against tax collector greed and intimidation, which, through a single misfortune, could reduce him to poverty, even slavery. And that wasn't all. Papa knew that Judah had introduced me to the art and science of alchemy, a pursuit my father regarded as unseemly, especially for a woman destined to run his investment business.

So to Papa, Judah was just another bastard with no prospects. A stream of sour breath would accompany his bitter words whenever the subject of Judah came up. He'd say, "I curse the day I ever sent you to collect his mortgage payment." Then he would stir the air with an accusing finger under my nose and say, "Remember who you are, Miriam, a well-educated Roman citizen." He'd space out his words when he said, "a Roman citizen," a privilege that had cost both sets of my grandparents small fortunes. To Papa, the purpose of marriage was to secure the future of the family. He'd say, "I'm already forty years old, and your brother is too busy ogling every prostitute waiting for a legionnaire at the Gate of the Sun. So all my hopes rest on you."

But time arranges all things. Papa died, and then four years ago, when Judah had paid off the mortgage on his shop and bought Roman citizenship, he asked me to marry him.

* * *

The wrought iron grille across the entrance to Judah's shop was closed and locked, but he'd left the heavy wooden shutters open. I pinched some color into my cheeks, smoothed my flyaway hair, and then took a few minutes to watch him as he stood before his workbench, rewinding a spool of wire and storing the metal scraps in an earthenware *cantharus*, a two-handled drinking cup. When I reached through the grille and knocked on the shutters, he greeted me with a smile that rivaled moonlight on the Nile. And then, as he threaded around his display cases, he grabbed the long wooden key that hung from a hook on the wall, unlocked the grille, and pushed it open for me before relocking it. And all the while, I had the pleasure of watching the folds of his workingman's tunic whisper across his thighs.

"Did you come all this way to flirt with the most famous jeweler in the world?" he asked, raising his eyebrows in mock inquiry.

"You want to know the truth?"

"No, I want to hear that you can't stand being away from me."

"Well, that's true, but the fact is I'm here on serious business. About a ring."

"You know I'd gladly make one for you—"

"No, it's about a ring you made for someone else."

"Uh-oh, I can see you're burning with jealousy!" He shook his finger at me with naughty delight. "Come into my office so I can serve you some tea and you can tell me all about it."

The fantasies I'd had as a young woman about that sanctum at the back of his shop! When at long last, he'd ushered me behind that scrim to show me the samples of copper he'd been heating with seeds of silver, I had to chuckle at how fanciful my imagination had been. His cubicle was so spartan with only the light from a louvered east-facing window and the simplest furnishings: a wooden sleeping couch; washstand, pitcher, and basin; a table and chair; and two raw pine shelves that held all else he owned.

After our marriage, he converted that space into an office dominated by an oblong cedar desk and cushioned chair beneath rows of neatly labeled cubbies for his records, but he kept the original table and chair. Best of all, he'd added a charcoal-burning cooking furnace recessed into a marble-topped counter to keep a steady fire under a sputtering kettle.

I slumped into the chair, my forearms dissolving onto my thighs, while Judah reached for the kettle and a tower of nested glassware to present me with a cup of mint tea. Then, after refilling the kettle with water from a hydria on the counter, he pushed away some scrolls from the edge of his desk and sat there, one leg dangling while the other rested on the floor.

Bending over the teacup, the steam caressed my face before I let the brew tickle the roof of my mouth and slide down my throat in waves of delight. When only a puddle remained, I set the teacup down, swiveled around to face him, and got right to the point. "I'm here about a woman you made a ring for. She's been kidnapped." Despite the tea, a chill went right through me. "The kidnappers threaten to burn her alive if the ransom is not deposited in the Bank of Gabinius by the end of today. One of your clients gave his wife that ring shortly after they moved to Alexandria. Her portrait in mosaics is set in malachite. I need to know who they are."

A fan of deep lines sprung up between his brows as, rubbing his chin, he closed his eyes to plunge into his sea of memories and paddle through them. Some impression must have bobbed to the surface because his eyes snapped open, and he nodded. "That was a few years ago. His wife came in twice, first for me to sketch her face and then to have the ring fitted."

"How is it that you remember her?"

"She had the kind of features that stick in your memory. Not that she was attractive except in a vulgar sort of way—blood-red stiletto nails, overplucked eyebrows arched over lustful eyes, and a thicket of impossibly bright, blade-straight orangish hair. I had a problem though." He began nodding even before finishing his sentence. "She had the long face of an underfed horse, but given her vanity, I knew she'd never accept the ring unless I compressed her forehead, padded her cheekbones, and raised her chin. On the ring, of course. My issue was how much could I alter her face and still have her marvel at its likeness."

"So, who was she?"

"I'll check." Extending his body like a ladder, he withdrew a scroll from one of his cubbies and placed it on his desk.

His back curving over the scroll, he unrolled it about halfway. His eyes followed his forefinger as it slid down the panel. "Ah, here it is: Quintus Valens Cinnus, retired legionnaire, and his wife Drusa. Living on Lake Mareotis." Looking up, he added, "Probably near the papyrus factories along the shoreline." Turning back to a note squeezed in the margin, he thumped his forefinger on that entry. "Ordered the ring three years ago, on the tenth day before the calends of May, and my assistant delivered it on the *nones* of July. Here's a copy of the receipt signed and dated by Drusa with her description of the ring." Shoulders squared and eyebrows lifted, he asked in a voice thick with exaggerated pride, "Anything else, my dear?"

"Great job. Of course, I'd expect nothing less from the most famous jeweler in the world, who even presents his clients with a receipt on vellum to sign, but I do have one question."

"Only one from the most famous detective in the world?"

"Well, just one for now. Why did it take so long, more than two months, to make the ring?"

"Pirates. Attacking the gold shipments from Spain. Before our military transports began carrying the ingots."

"Makes sense. Do you remember anything else about the couple?"

"So, you did have another question! Actually, I've told you all I can about her. Her husband, on the other hand, looked and sounded like what he must have been: a leather-faced, bull-necked soldier with a loud voice. But by the time he retired and came into the shop, he doddered in with a forward stoop, lugging the burden of his age on rounded shoulders and spindly legs."

We were silent for a while, allowing the moan of the surf, the cry of the gulls, and the faint toll of a buoy to fill the space between us.

"Anyways, why the interest?" he asked, opening his hands as if to free a butterfly.

I shrugged with my best attempt at a cryptic smile.

Judah's face squeezed into a heavy frown. "Miriam, I asked you a question with words. Please answer me that way."

I would have told a lie if I could have thought of one fast enough. Instead, I told the truth. "Professor Jason asked me to assist him, perhaps because—"

"Uh-oh, I knew it!" he exclaimed, throwing up his hands. "You know how it disturbs me when you get involved with crimin—"

"But you and I agreed—"

"I know, I know, and I do all I can to support your mission—as you support mine, but—"

"I'll be careful."

"Please," he said with a worried edge.

"Promise. I just have one more favor to ask. I want to borrow the receipt for Drusa's ring. Just for one day. I'll return it tomorrow."

Judah closed his eyes with a sigh and nodded.

Having dealt at least temporarily with that recurring source of contention between us, we rolled to our feet, his clenched teeth betraying the strain, my muscles stiff from tension. But with his protective hand on my shoulder as he guided me toward the grille, I felt satisfied with the information I'd gotten. Until I remembered that the kidnappers would burn Drusa alive tomorrow.

Chapter Five: Aquila (aka Binyamin)

To tell you the truth, it felt good being back at The Pegasus. I'd stayed here as a kid, waiting those endless days for the ship's herald to announce its departure for Ostia. Of course, Sergius had told me there'd be no way to predict that date. Between the winds and a million fuckin' omens like some magpie perching on the rigging or some asshole dreaming of an owl, it was a wonder any ship sailed at all. So, no way could I be a sea captain! When I wanna go, I go. Period. So yeah, I remembered the thrill of that first leg of my trip to Capua and my escape from the battleground that was my boyhood with Papa! And me, just sixteen years old, laying eyes on The Pegasus, the old inn squatting at the end of a maze of rutted alleys and gutters, beyond the sign with that winged horse springing from Medusa's womb. But I couldn't help wishing I'd have sprung from my own mother's womb that way.

Well, that time was my first at The Pegasus. Now was different. I was loafing on a lumpy cot in a low-raftered, windowless attic *cella* with an upright beam in the center supporting the worm-eaten baulk of timber that was the roof. But at least now I was waiting for another kind of ship to come in, my ship of fortune. Ha! Anyways, the horniest broad in the city and me were sweating out the afternoon with only the dim light from a smoking oil lamp hanging from a joist and a few darts of sunlight shooting through a hole in the roof.

But I had to set that broad straight. *"Ma Zeus*, will you shut your fuckin' mouth? I can't stand your bellyaching another minute!"

"My poor, poor darling," she said with a simper. "I just hate being cooped up in this rat hole."

"Look, I smuggle in food from the public room. What more do you want?"

"Food? Is that what you call it? The soup alone is enough to saw off the roof of my mouth."

"Hey, you're supposed to be a hostage, and I'm supposed to be torturing you with hot coals." I squawked with laughter, rocking back and forth, spittle flowing from my mouth till it soaked into the mattress ticking. "Am I a genius or what for adding that touch?"

"What touch?"

"The hot coals, fish brain! Besides, The Pegasus is perfect. No one you know would ever come across you here. So, shut up, will you? I'll get the dough today.

"Any sign of it?"

"Quit asking me that! It's there." That was when a nasty little taunt rose up sharp as a blade on my tongue. "Hey, you sure your precious Quintus even wants you back?" *It's only been four days, and I'm already sick of you.* "And you sure your mangy old soldier's got that kind of dough? 'Cause someone could have already given Charon a little help ferrying him across the river. Hey, you never know. So, you and the kid—"

"Tullus. His name is Tullus—"

"Yeah. So, you and the kid get it all?"

"Why can't you remember my son's name?"

That's when my loathing for her hit me like a swarm of locusts. *Bam!* I slapped her so hard she spun across the *cella*, blood gushing from her nose. "I told you to shut the fuck up. I need that stake to buy the *ludus*. Then we'll be the richest and most famous couple in Alexandria. Who knows? Maybe the empire."

Shutting her up like that, even for a second, felt good. But there she was, yukking it up again.

"You keep talking about our being rich, but all I really want is to be with you. Why can't we just run away?"

"You crazy bitch! I'm getting so sick a' telling you. What would we live on? You think Quintus will continue my salary and your allowance? Ha! Besides, I got it all planned. Sergius is gonna recruit new hires for me. Didn't I tell you that's how he recruited me? I'll bet that mothafuckah can already smell the fees coming out of my ransom money. You gonna see him send me the best *lanistae* and *doctores*."

"The best what?"

"You really don't know shit, do you? The *lanistae* manage the gladiators, and the *doctores* train them.

"*Lanistae* manage. *Doctores* train. *Lanistae… Doctores*."

There she went mumbling again, doing everything to make me crazy.

"I'll try to remember. I promise." I swear she looked into her palm and bobbed her head as if writing it down with her eyes.

"Here, this ought to keep it in that skull of yours." I stung her a little north of her temple with a few nothing taps, one, two, three. So big deal, her knees buckled a little.

"Hey, stop that!"

"What did I do? Is it my fault you got lousy knees? *Tsk, tsk.* Anyways, what are you gonna do about it? We're on this hook together."

"There's only one place I want your hands." She licked her lips and lifted each breast, one ripe melon in each hand, and that hunger for her came on me like a fire.

Chapter Six: Miriam

The sinking sun shot its last spit of light into Judah's eyes as he passed through the archway from the atrium into our dining room. Calisto had already positioned two of the three dining couches so they were parallel to the window. They faced each other across a low ivory table with its legs carved in the figure of a squatting griffin. I flanked each couch with a pair of enameled ebony lampstands, measured their distance from the couch with my forearm to perfect the symmetry, and lit the oil lamps with the fire steel hanging from one of the lampstands.

But as the darkness pressed against the window, even the glow from the lampstands and songs of the nightbirds did little to dispel my sense of doom. And so a queer chill was all I felt as I signaled Calisto to bring us a freshly mixed krater of wine, a basket of pita, and the first course, chilled cucumber slices in a tangy dill dressing.

"We're not going to talk about my case tonight, are we?" I asked as I ladled the wine into our goblets. I took a sip and gazed at Judah over the rim.

"Not unless you want to. But I am curious what you did with the names of the kidnapped woman and her husband."

"I took a chance that Bion would be in his shop. I was hoping he could tell me something about the kidnappers by studying the ransom note."

Bion, Phoebe's husband, used to be a public slave repairing scrolls in the workshop of the Great Library. There he developed an expertise in assessing the various grades of papyrus as well as analyzing the handwriting on the panels. And so he became useful when the scholars needed to identify the canonical version of a classical text or when they suspected a text could be a forgery.

Eventually Bion was sold to a Jewish sandal-maker and bibliophile in Caesarea who liberated him after six years as is the custom of our people. Along with the quitclaim, his master gave him enough money to establish a business repairing and selling rare manuscripts. Now Bion owns the most prosperous *bibliopōleion* in our agora, where he deals in classical manuscripts as well as the works of contemporary scholars like Thrasyllus of Mendes and engineers like our very own Hero. With his connections to the Great Library and sunny disposition, his business has thrived.

"Well, did you find out anything from Bion?" Judah asked.

"Let's start on the cucumbers first."

⁂ ⁂ ⁂

By the time I fished out a stray sprig of dill, popped it into my mouth, and licked my top lip, Judah had scooped up a loaf of pita, torn it in half, and filled it with cucumbers. I waited for him to take a big bite and swallow a few sips of wine before beginning.

"Judging by his suppressed yawn, Bion had probably been napping in his office when I called to him through the grille of his shop. Maneuvering his paunch with the skill of a sea captain, he sailed around the half-empty boxes of scrolls and stationery supplies to greet me with an easy smile that turned his gold-flecked eyes into fringed slits and his chubby cheeks into pomegranates.

"'I have a question only you can answer,' I said.

"'Sounds important,' he replied, as he gestured me in with an arm roll.

"I hadn't seen Bion in more than two years since a rare edition of Menander's *Dyskolos* displayed in a vitrine at the front of his shop had been stolen. When I'd asked how much the scroll was worth, his voice had dropped to a whisper. 'About 2000 drachmas,' he'd said, 'enough to buy the grandest mansion in Alexandria.'

"Bion was a tad plumper judging by the heavily tooled leather belt girding him where his waist had once been. Pearls of flesh peeked out between the coin-like bronze buttons that fastened the sides of his heavily embroidered linen tunic. But the elegant simplicity of his office at the back of the shop hadn't changed at all.

"Two Herodian oil lamps on the marble-topped cabinets framing the lone east-facing window were the only challenge to the afternoon shadows. Each throwing a hoop of golden light, they sputtered a greeting in the rush of air as we passed through the scrim.

"'How good to see you, Miriam,' he said and motioned for me to take a seat across from him at the long rosewood table that dominated the center of his office. Then, resting his palms on his knees, he waited in a deep listening silence.

"'First I must apologize for bursting in without an appoint—'

"He waved his hand to brush away my words.

"'—ment. My only excuse is that the answer is vital to the life of an innocent woman and her husband. Second, I ask that our meeting be kept confidential. I'm here about a case, but I learned of it only indirectly and have already violated my own oath to keep the particulars secret.

"'And finally, I apologize for mentioning the need for discretion. More than anyone, you have proved your trustworthiness time and time again, beginning in Caesarea, of course, but especially when the Torah mantle was desecrated in the Great Synagogue.'

"His eyes sparkled with pride. Then fitting his palms together, he steepled his forefingers and pressed them against his rosebud lips.

"'I have two documents, this jeweler's receipt and a scrap of papyrus, both purportedly penned in part by the same woman. I need to know what you can tell me about her.'"

Judah shifted on his couch and propped up his elbows with a cushion. I thought he might say something, but he didn't. So, I continued:

"The shadows painted blotches on the table and splashed the oriental carpet with ragged pools of darkness. As I reached into my satchel for the ransom note and the receipt, Bion brought over the lamps to spread a skin of light across the table. Then he placed the documents side-by-side. Hunching over the table, his forearms balancing on its edge, he eyed them, first one, then the oth—"

"Slow down, Miriam," said Judah, raking his hands through his wreath of curls. "You didn't tell me anything about a ransom note."

"Sorry, my mind keeps bouncing from one thread to the next. The kidnappers had sent a ransom demand to Quintus Valens Cinnus. In it, they threatened to kill his wife if an enormous sum wasn't deposited in the Bank of Gabinius by the end of the day today. I myself became curious about the note because it was written on such a refined grade of papyrus. I figured Bion could tell me its provenance."

Judah slowly emptied his goblet, never taking his eyes off me.

"Second, Valens Cinnus said he recognized his wife's handwriting on the note, something about the elegant rounding of the letters. So, I wanted Bion to confirm that the ransom note and receipt were written by the same woman. But most of all, I wanted Bion to compare the two samples and tell me whether she was under stress when she put her pen to either document."

"Got it." Judah nodded and then said, "Okay, go on."

"So Bion examined both documents. 'Before I examine them with the globe,' he explained, 'I want to get an overall impression of each document. They're very different, of course. The receipt was written on the flesh side of the skin of a stillborn calf. I can tell by the fine white appearance of the vellum, which contrasts so strikingly with the ink, not that the ink is unusual, just a blend of lamp-black, gum, and water. No indication of the ink running, so the skin must have been treated, maybe with pumice or lime. I just can't tell…'

"While giving a running account of his observations, Bion's speech began to slow, his diction to slur until he was speaking only to himself, his voice hardly a mumble before it dribbled into silence. But you know me. Words of impatience burned in my throat—"

"I've even heard them burn aloud a few times," said Judah as his words sifted through his mouthful of cucumbers.

"*Shsh!* Where was I?… Oh, now I remember. It seemed like Bion was taking forever to examine the receipt, but his silence couldn't have lasted that long. Minutes later, once he picked up the scrap, his voice stirred again as the words rolled out of his mouth.

"'Now this scrap comes from a sheet of the highest grade of Egyptian papyrus. Surely it was manufactured in one of the workshops along Lake Mareotis. The writing is on the recto side—'

"He looked up to explain that the recto side is the front side of a sheet of papyrus, the preferred side, so the writing runs parallel to rather than across the grain.

"I appreciated Bion's thoroughness, but my heart was kicking against my chest. I just wanted to know whether Drusa had written the first part of that note.

"Shifting his weight, Bion picked up both documents and one of the lamps, pivoted out of his chair, pushed it back under the table with his paunch, and scooted over to the workbench along the northern wall of his office. Planting first the lamp on his workbench and then his feet in an isosceles stance astride the stool, he reached to the shelf above him for a globe so he could scrutinize the receipt and scrap of papyrus.

"Nibbling at my cuticles, I was otherwise poised like a statue. Barely breathing, perched on the edge of the chair, leaning forward, gripping the edge of the table until the knuckles of my free hand turned white.

"The wait seemed interminable, but when I looked down, none of the carpet's pools of darkness had shifted.

"Meanwhile Bion was taking turns stooping over the workbench, his nose almost touching the globe. Then leaning back, he lifted each document to catch a sliver of light. Pursing his lips, then biting them, he creased his brow, rubbed the back of his neck, and scratched his head. Finally, nodding decisively, he shelved the globe, turned to me, and spoke with authority:

"'Look, based on the handwriting, I'd say the receipt was penned by a literate woman well past her youth, writing with the finest *calamus*, probably bronze and custom-made for her hand. Moreover, the nib was sharp, possibly gold. There are no nicks on the vellum, which suggests that she was not under stress when she wrote it.'

"'And the scrap of papyrus?'

"'Same hand. Same *calamus*. Despite the cramping, the letters show the same odd rounding, but with the globe, I can see a slight tremor in her broad strokes. So yes, she was under mild stress, more likely from being rushed rather than from being nervous or afraid. The rest of the writing was done by a semi-literate man using a reed pen, one that needed to be sharpened, which confirms my impression that he too was in a hurry.'

"With a deep inhale, Bion squared his shoulders and continued. 'Yes, he was definitely in a hurry. Look at the gray splotches on the papyrus. The nib must have leaked, but he didn't bother to blot the ink. So, while I cannot tell you who penned this scrap of papyrus, I can say with reasonable certainty that it was written by a woman first, the same woman who penned the receipt, and then by a man, and both were pressed for time.'"

With that, I turned to Judah, my mouth suddenly dry. "So, you see, my darling, I've stepped into a most bizarre crime."

* * *

I passed the night in my sitting room, weary but restive as I brooded over unanswered questions, inventing a hundred explanations for why Drusa hadn't been afraid. Most were absurd, some even impossible. Just as dawn was edging the walls with a pale glow, I heard in the stillness the *whoosh* of Calisto's skirt and the echo of her light steps hurrying down the tessellated stairs into the atrium. Despite the pull of fatigue, I managed to don a long, sleeveless tunic over my rumpled *capitium*, the light chemise I wear for sleeping. And then the *thwack* of my own feet in pursuit filled the air like a small parade.

My vision blurred through gritty lids. I nevertheless caught a glimpse of Calisto as she received Professor Jason at the front door and showed him into my study.

"Please, I must see …uh…Miss bat Isaac…uh… right away," he muttered, this time his diction careless, so different from what I'd heard just three days ago.

Directly behind Calisto at the doors to my office, almost bumping into her as she turned to fetch me, I mouthed for her to bring us some lavender tea right away.

"Forgive me for …*hmm* disturbing you before full light, and this time…uh… with no notice at all."

My lips flickered with the faintest curve of commiseration as I nodded, sat behind my desk, and suppressing a yawn, pointed to one of the *curule* chairs. "Have a seat, Professor."

The emotion that accompanied him was evident in more than the gloom that clouded his eyes. His sunken face, smudged with whiskers in its hollows, was more deeply furrowed than ever. For an elongated moment, oblivious to having been addressed, he stared into the well of darkness that was the peristyle before turning and plodding slump-shouldered toward one of the chairs, all the while clutching the edge of my desk. At last, letting go, he stumbled into the chair, gripping its low arms with trembling hands. Whatever misfortune had brought him to me had stamped him with its grimness.

I resisted reeling off my usual platitudes. Instead, I kept silent as I gazed at the grief-shattered face across my desk.

He swallowed hard. Tears thickened in his eyes before trickling down his withered face and leaving glossy tracks of sorrow. Then his head sank into his hands as a flood of tears filtered through his fingers.

My nerves buzzing with dread, I nevertheless waited for his breathing to normalize, for some of the pain to drain out of his soul. It couldn't have taken so long as it seemed, but he finally raised his head. And then he blinked away a lingering tear and wiped his blotched face with his palms. Still, the sadness clung to him.

"My faithful friend, Quintus—it doesn't matter now that I tell you his name—Quintus Valens Cinnus. Perhaps you've heard of him. Or at least his late cousin Sextus Afranius Burrus, prefect to Nero's Praetorian Guard." He squeezed his eyes shut and opened them again, but they seemed focused elsewhere, as if he were looking inward. Then he spoke in a quavering whisper. "My old school chum and rival at the gymnasium... my match in combat sports like *pankration*, a combination of—"

"I know. Of boxing and wrestling. My brother—"

"He'll never walk this sweet Earth again! Struck down yesterday by some sick scoundrel. Left to die, bleaching in the sun like a common thief. And the worst part, I couldn't save him," he said, blubbering like a child. "This fearless man on the battlefield was too afraid to let me even try. Why didn't I coax him more? Or even break my pledge of secrecy? What harm would it have done compared to this?" he asked as shame, guilt, and sorrow competed for purchase on his face.

And shouldn't I have done the same thing, compelled the professor to tell me what he knew? Instead, I imposed on Phoebe, Bion, even Judah and Orestes, all for naught. Despite the spurt of acid firing into my gorge, I rose from behind my desk to sit next to him on the other *curule* chair. He shifted his own weight, crossing and recrossing his legs as was his habit, while I angled my body toward his and grasped his hands.

"I can see he meant a lot to you."

"No matter where he was, whatever his military campaign, we kept in touch. We even met in Rome a few times when he was on furlough and I could take leave from the medical school. He escorted me everywhere: to the best restaurants, the Theater of Marcellus, and of course, the *Circus Maximus* for the chariot races. How he got us seats at the southeastern turn, I'll never know, but we had the best view of the 'shipwrecks.' That's what they call the crashes, when the driver, horses, and chariot in one thrilling moment turn into a tangled wreckage of bones, blood, and splinters.

"I can still remember the Theater of Pompey, where Caesar was assassinated. And as if that wasn't enough, he introduced me to his cousin Burrus, who along with Seneca the Younger, was the emperor's closest advisor. I probably could have gotten an audience with Nero himself had I asked. That's how good Quintus was to me.

"Oh, what's the use?" he muttered, raking his hand through his hair. "He was the best friend I ever had." His lips tightened into a long white scar as he shook his head in disbelief. "We grew up with all the other privileged kids in the *Palatium*, right around the corner from the *Domus Augusti*. His family was richer than mine, but he willingly shared his opportunities with me as long, of course, as I shared my homework with him." A little chuckle escaped from his lips before turning into a sob.

"So, tell me about yesterday," I urged. Anything to change the subject. Besides, my fatigue was quickly turning into exasperation. Only by digging my nails into my palms could I squelch the churning in my innards to listen for a connection between the murder and the kidnapping.

The professor uncrossed his legs like the blades of a scissors and leaned forward. "When a maid noticed yesterday that my friend hadn't appeared for his noon meal, she sent the bearers to look for him, first on the estate and then along the lake. Lake Mareotis. That's where Quintus lives. I mean lived. Where he took his morning swim. When the bearers saw his body floating in the lake, one of them went to the magistrate, who sent a soldier to fish him out and then notified me."

A soft tap on the door jamb and Calisto entered with two glasses of tea. She placed each on an Indian cotton napkin beside us on my desk. My visitor picked his up and paused, gazing into it as he might have stared into the surface of the lake. Then he put it down as if too distracted to take a sip. I slowly emptied my glass while eyeing him over the lip until he was ready to continue.

"The soldier reported it as a death by drowning. Of course, I'll do the autopsy this afternoon to determine the definitive cause of death. My friend was a great athlete and fine swimmer even as a boy. So I knew he couldn't have simply drowned. Sure enough, when I did an onsite examination, I saw the fracture in his left sphenoid bone. Along with its central position and articulations with other bones of the skull, it provides for the skull's rigidity to—"

"To protect the brain and nerves." My fingers were already pleating the folds in my tunic to fend off the impatience sprouting inside me.

"Yes. So, he must have been hit with something, perhaps something as ordinary as a sharp rock."

"How terrible that must have been for you. I mean to see him like that, but can you tell me whether the ransom had been paid before

Quintus was killed?"

His eyes flashed with annoyance. "How can that matter now? Either way, my friend is dead."

"Please, Professor. It matters."

"Well, since you ask, the chatty clerk at the Bank of Gabinius, the one with the long ear lobes, told me yesterday morning that Quintus had been there earlier to transfer money to another account. In fact, he said the amount was so substantial that he had to get the head clerk to approve the transaction." A pucker settled on his brow as he rubbed the back of his neck. "Why is that important?"

"It means that if the kidnappers killed Quintus, collecting the ransom wasn't their only motive."

And that's when it all made sense to me: the evidence from Binyamin, Abasi, Judah, and Bion. So, with a feeling of concentrated excitement, I called for Orestes as soon as I could usher the professor out the door.

Chapter Seven: Aquila (aka Binyamin)

Selene, that ferret-face hostess at the fuckin' Pegasus. It was all her fault. Too bad. I'd gotten rather used to the place, especially its food. At least, it was better than the stew we'd get at the *ludus*. *Sagina* they called it, but it was more like the slop you feed livestock. Gives you a lot of gas but reduces bleeding. At least that's what all those assholes say.

Anyways, you can't miss Selene, that good-for-nothing whore with the flabby jawline, sagging breasts, and the stink of lead paste, which she slaps on her nose to cover the rose garden blooming there. Except it don't. Cover her nose, I mean. And come to think of it, you *can* miss her 'cause she skips out in the early afternoon. Always leaving her station, saying business is slow so she's taking an extended lunch. Ha! How come that's when I hear bedsprings squeaking through the walls?

I guess that's how Orestes snuck in. Then he must have banged on every door till he found me at the top of this garbage heap, where the heat was biting like it had teeth. Soon as I saw him, the dread stabbed me like a dagger. He sailed in to tell me my uppity sister wanted to talk to me about my future, what with the death of Quintus and all. My future! Like I was gonna have one!

Drusa's scream would have taken the paint off the walls had there been any. She was speechless, her mouth open like a fish thrashing on the deck. But not for long, her being speechless. Never was. "You pile of shit!" I swear she squawked like a gull on a rock. "What did you do that for?" Then, quick as a snake, she gripped my arm like a vice with those stiletto nails. Couldn't shake her off without losing some skin.

"So we could be together, you stupid cow, like we planned. Hey," I said, hammering my finger into her chest, "It looked like he was never gonna fork over the dough, remember? Without him, you and the brat can at least inherit—"

"Be together? No, no!" she shrieked, clawing back her hair, her eyes aflame. Then, with clenched fists, she leaped and whirled like a spooked horse. "Without his devoted father, who else will take care of my sweet boy?"

I couldn't believe her lashing out at me when she'd been sticking to me like a limpet. But as soon as Orestes left—I swear a rod was up his ass—she gathered some stuff—her fancy pen, jewelry, and himation— and was gone quicker than a thief in the night.

Well, let her eat shit.

Anyways, that's how I ended up at my know-it-all sister's house waiting on a bench like a fuckin' dog, my teeth rattling like a backroom dice game, not knowing what she was gonna pull next.

Chapter Eight: Miriam

"Miss Miriam, your brother is waiting to see you."

When I looked up from my desk, I saw the last of the day in the patterns of shade flickering on Calisto's serene face. Drawing in a deep breath to fortify myself, I pushed aside the ledger. I couldn't concentrate anyway. The numbers kept receding into a well of darkness.

I'd just gotten back from seeing Drusa at the family's estate on Lake Mareotis. The latest evidence from Orestes having cemented my suspicions into certainty, I knew I had to call on her if I ever expected to sleep again. That dread may have sent scalding rivulets of sweat down my back, but the visit with her was more chilling than I could have imagined.

Orestes and Solon had brought me there through the vine-woven, wrought iron gate and around the expansive formal gardens. There was no hint of the villa itself until we rounded the last curve of the sweeping brick drive. And then I beheld a jewel worthy of Poppaea Sabina, a perfectly symmetric colonnaded building, its mortised stones breathing in the scent of the rosemary hedges. And just as Abasi had said, the entrance was adorned with bronze doors, which looked to me as if they could have withstood an assault from Hannibal himself.

So too the doorkeeper was a grotesque caricature of a rat with his dark beady eyes, needle-like yellowish teeth, brown at the gum line, and upper front incisors overhanging his lower lip. When I explained that I'd come as a friend of Professor Jason to pay my respects, he emerged from his cage to lead me through a wide hall into the atrium, its paneled walls smelling of polish and carved with swirling vines. There I sat on a bench to wait for Drusa while listening in rapid succession to a rattle, a staccato of pings, and the bounce of a ball. When a child squealed, "Frogs in the well!" and then, "Mommy, I won!" I realized Drusa was playing knucklebones with her son. Then, with a murmur of endearment, she clapped her hands, presumably to call for a slave.

Instead of enjoying the apple-like scent of the chamomiles in planters around the *impluvium*, I tried to compose myself and rehearse once more the deal I hoped to make with her.

Of course, Drusa had had no inkling of who I was or why I'd come. Instead, her slippered feet *thwacked* into the atrium, appearing and disappearing under the skirt of her tunic. Acknowledging me with an irritated nod, she beckoned me with a bejeweled arm, and like a baby chick, I followed the *woosh* of her tunic and the jingle of her bracelets. But the loudest sound I heard was the acid gurgling in my stomach.

She led me into a marbled interior that was the library, its mahogany shelves crammed with scrolls, its vaulted ceiling frescoed with seabirds, and its free-standing urns pluming with freshly cut roses. Directing me to a chair inlaid with ivory, she folded herself into the bronze-faced couch across from me.

"I'm here, Drusa, because of your husband's death. My name is Miriam bat Isaac." Her impassive nod told me she had no idea who I was.

"I'm Aquila's sister."

A ragged intake of breath, her back straightening into a plumbline, she locked her arms across her chest as if to prepare herself for the worst.

I continued in a voice as smooth as custard. "I have evidence against you and Aquila for staging your kidnapping and murdering your husband, Quintus Valens Cinnus."

She shut her eyes, and then a moment later, her upper lip stretched wide in panic. She smacked her palm against the arm of the couch. "It was Aquila! Aquila did it! He kidnapped me, and when my husband wouldn't pay the ransom, he killed him. If I hadn't escaped, he would have killed—"

I held up my palms before any more lies could grow in her mouth. "Drusa, I told you I have evidence. I know your husband paid the ransom. Moreover, the man who dropped in on you and Aquila was my bearer, Orestes. He came to alert my brother that I knew all about Quintus's death."

"Well," she said, throwing up her hands. "Doesn't that prove I knew nothing about it? Besides, why should I believe anything you say?"

"My bearer knew he'd find you both at The Pegasus. Aquila was familiar with that inn, and it was near The Lizard's Tail, where he hired the courier to bring the ring and ransom note to your husband. What's more, that courier is ready to identify Aquila." *Well, that might be a stretch, but a* denarius *or two could surely refresh his memory of the man with the scars and tattoos.* "Whether or not you had foreknowledge of the murder of your husband—and I suspect you didn't—you were complicit in faking the kidnapping that led to his murder. Not only can Orestes attest to that, but it was you who wrote most of the ransom note. Both your husband and a handwriting expert identified the script as yours."

A flare of alarm glittered in her eyes. "This is madness! Aquila made me write it," she shrieked. "He held a dagger to my neck and said if I couldn't convince Quintus that my life was in danger, he'd watch the blood pump out of my throat until the *cella* looked like a slaughterhou—"

"No, Drusa." I leaned into her, close enough for the sour smell of her desperation to filter up my nose. "Your life wasn't in danger. The evidence doesn't support that. My expert not only confirmed that you penned the ransom note, but other than your being in a hurry, your handwriting showed no sign of stress."

That was when, with pearls of spittle gleaming on her lips and her features swelling, she sprang from the couch and spoke in a voice heavy with menace. "Listen, Miss Whoever-you-are, I have a house full of slaves ready to kill you whenever I say the word."

The urge to grab a clump of that outrageous hair rose in my gullet as my chest inflated with rage, but I managed to keep my voice as cool as a twilight breeze. "*Tsk, tsk.* Killing me won't do you any good," I said, shaking my head. "The evidence is safe with Professor Jason." Okay, so I lied again.

She slapped my face.

I guess my brother never told her that he'd taught me to box. With my cheek smarting, I moved in, pushing through a flurry of clawing hands. I watched her feet, measured her reach, and drove a fist into her belly. The flesh was soft, flabbier than I expected. She doubled over. One more punch, an uppercut too fast for her to see, and her nose opened up like a rotten pomegranate. Then, as soon as she raised her hands to stop the rope of blood gushing from her face, I stung her with one more body punch. That was all it took. Her knees buckled, and she dropped to the floor.

"Please," she begged in a fear-clotted whisper, groveling at my feet, her reddish hair like a pool of blood on the floor. "I'll do anything you say. Just don't take my boy from me." A strangled sob and she continued. "He needs a mother, and Quintus's brothers, with the help of Seneca the Younger, will petition the courts to take him away from me."

That was what I meant by chilling. Drusa would have abandoned her son for the very man she was quick to blame for murdering her husband. But soon after, she was ready to hide behind that son to save herself from the charge of staging her own kidnapping.

At least now she was ready to listen to the deal I came to offer.

* * *

"You came for a reason. You better tell me what you want." Drusa's gaze was steady, but her voice trembled.

She seemed to have gotten smaller. We sat facing each other as before, except now her hands were stained crimson, and her tunic was streaked with blood.

"Yes, I want something, and I think it would be to your advantage as well." I took the next moment to let some of the fury drain out of me. Soon enough, we'd be partners in our own web of deceit.

"First, I have to say I have only contempt for what you and my brother did." Then, with half-lidded eyes, I spelled it out. "You swindled your husband, your son's devoted father, for your own insatiable lust and my brother's boundless greed. And because of you, a loving man's—even a noble man's—life was snuffed out with a savage ferocity."

I waited awhile before continuing.

A taut silence filled the air.

I could hear the buzz of a single fly.

The words piled up on my tongue

Until I punched through the silence.

"But to let the wheels of justice turn would take the life of my brother, who grew up knowing only bitter reprimands and a never-ending series of harsh punishments. And at the same time, it would deprive your son of his only parent and burden him forever with the nodding heads and wagging fingers of scandalmongers."

Drusa's eyes began to swim, but she didn't sob. Instead, she covered her face with her palms and wept softly while the tears trickled through her fingers.

I waited for her to swallow and take a deep breath. Then she dried her face with the hem of her tunic.

"As much as I deplore what my brother has done, he is still my brother." I shuddered, remembering all the blame he'd had to shoulder. His only defense was to build a wall of indifference to the feelings of others. And to some extent, I was responsible for that callousness by continuing to aid and abet his childish pranks, tall tales, and misdeeds."

Drusa clutched her bejeweled necklace and kept watching my expression as she pressed the beads to her lips.

"Of course, Tullus would suffer if you're executed, but as a citizen of Rome, you could expect a presumably painless death by beheading."

Her mouth hinged open; her face paralyzed with terror.

"The outcome for my brother would not be so benign. See, a gladiator must renounce his citizenship upon joining a *ludus*. Aquila was able to reclaim his rights when he was discharged from the one in Capua. But having left the *ludus* in Alexandria before fulfilling his contract"—I didn't mention that he left in a coffin—"he lost the right to regain that precious status. So, he'd be forced to die either by crucifixion or, if games are scheduled for that day, by *damnatio ad bestia.*"

"*Damnatio*, what?"

"You heard me. *Ad bestia.* Condemned to the wild beasts. Thrown to the lions. And why not?" I added, feigning indifference with my palms out. "It's fast, it entertains, and at the same time serves as an appalling warning to others."

Despite her efforts to conceal her agitation, a low animal moan escaped from her lips, now as white as a fish's belly.

"Therefore, for the sake of my brother's wretched past and your son's bright future, I am offering to suppress the evidence I have. I will ask Professor Jason to report that your Quintus hit his head on a boulder in the lake and died a natural albeit unfortunate death by drowning."

Drusa began to cry again, this time without restraint. Sobbing and slobbering, she sucked in gulps of air as her chest heaved. Her raw tears left gritty tracks on her crumpled face while her mouth sputtered saliva and her nose dripped silver threads onto the bodice of her tunic.

At last, her sobs eased to a whimper, and she wiped her red-rimmed eyes until they were glazed with only a watery film and smudged with the kohl she used to line her eyes.

I felt a prick of tears behind my own eyes but blinked them away before she could see a flare of pity there.

"But you must do something in return," I said.

Perching on the edge of the cushion now and leaning toward me, she nodded as if she had a choice.

"First, to honor the memory of your husband, atone for your transgressions, and make a feeble attempt at amends, you must take out of your own household funds a sum equal to double the ransom demand and donate it to the soup kitchens of Alex—"

Her hands fluttered like the wings of a panicked bird. "But I—"

I silenced her with a raised hand and an insistent voice. "Second, I believe my brother can still find goodness in his soul. And so for your own penance as well as his future, you must establish—again from your own household funds—an account for him equal to half the sum deposited for the kidnappers. You see, one of the conditions I'll impose on him will be that he'll have to leave the empire forever. This capital will serve as a safety net for his new life. Your husband gave the money to save your life. Now you must give half that to save my brother's."

She caved in as if I'd put my foot on her chest.

I delivered my closing like a bludgeon, each word uttered in the magisterial tone I'd rehearsed: "This agreement will require three signatures: yours, mine, and my brother's. Orestes will bring the document to Professor Jason's office in the Museum tomorrow morning. Thereafter you can sign it. When all of us have signed, the professor will keep it in a private repository. If you and my brother adhere to your respective pledges, then I promise to hold back the evidence that would surely condemn you both to death."

Her face haggard and weary, she sighed with resignation. She knew I could have demanded so much more.

And so I stood, wincing as I straightened my back before turning on my heels and showing myself out.

Chapter Nine: Miriam

"Did you forget, Miss Miriam? Your brother is waiting for you."

"Oh, I must have dozed off for a few minutes."

Except I hadn't. I'd been reliving my visit with Drusa, stirring the details to the surface like the bubbles of decay in the canal. And I'd lost more than a few minutes. I could already sense the darkness and hear the fearful screeches of an owl fill the night.

To pull back the shadows, Calisto lit a few lanterns and scattered the patches of light about my study. When my eyes became accustomed to the checkered light, I asked her to invite Binyamin in, and then she vanished with the quickness of a cat.

As soon as he pushed open the doors, I caught his stink, odors clashing with odors, the stench of his morning's *henket* vying with the ammoniac reek of old sweat, fermented semen, and the breath of a latrine. I drew back, feigning a cough to mask my retch. He looked like a bear shaken from hibernation, his brawny arms arcing out, his jowls bloated and smeared with stubble, his hair as scruffy as a tattered string mop, and his swollen eyelids deep in sockets half-mooned with purple.

Striding in with his usual cockiness, he took one of the *curule* chairs as if he owned it and turned it away from my desk. There he sat tall, erect, and motionless, flaunting a pretense of confidence with his hands on his hips and his shoulders inflated. I joined him in the matching chair and moved in close until his sour breath was in my mouth and his shadow was looming over me.

For the moment, we exchanged glances like actors, each having forgotten whose turn it was to speak. But then, ready to taunt, he cut through the silence.

"Okay, Miss Smarty-Pants, so you were onto me, but you weren't shrewd enough to stop me from killing him, were you? Ha!"

His scorn, unleashed in an acrid stream with narrowed eyes, reminded me of Papa. In that instant, I realized who'd taught Binyamin to be a bully. But I merely closed my eyes, pursed my lips, and waggled my head.

"Don't start with me, Binny. I'm not going to bandy words with you."

With a sarcastic smile that was more of a sneer, he hissed at me like a viper. Otherwise he didn't move; he just sat there, staring above my head with the empty gaze of a shark.

"I've asked you here to offer you a chance for a future, probably your only chance."

When his eyes locked onto mine, they felt like needles.

"You are my brother after all, my twin brother. Yes, I've despised your choices. So, I must have seemed like your enemy. But I was afraid for you just the same. I've always wanted a good life for you."

And then, as if my warehouse of memories had been illuminated by a bolt of lightning, I recognized a sobering truth. "I understand now, Binny, that we were reared to be rivals so Papa could use me as his deputy. I'm so sorry I never saw our childhood like that before—not that I think he did either. And I was simply relieved to be in his good graces."

"Ancient history!" he shouted. But with another "Ha!"—this one muted—he angled his body ever so slightly toward mine.

"I had no childhood, Sis, 'cause I had no parents, no mother, no father, only a vengeful tyrant too fuckin' enraged to heal himself."

He dug his fingertips into his eyes as if to tap a reservoir of strength lurking there.

"Truth is I don't even know what a father is. The closest I ever got was Sergius. True, he only helped when it was good for him—and he made plenty of dough off me—but at least he was there when I needed him. So yeah, I never had what you'd call a childhood."

"Listen, Binny, you know you'll have to leave the empire. You've killed a Roman warrior, a decorated hero, a cousin to Burrus, the prefect to Nero's Praetorian Gu—"

"Yeah, I know, and I'm too old for the *ludus* anyways, even to train the volunteers."

I felt my shoulders relax for the first time since his arrival. "But you're not too old to start a new life—a good life—in a place beyond Nero's reach. I can get the evidence against you suppressed—from the courier who delivered the ransom demand and from the autopsy of Quintus's body. And I'll see that you get a substantial sum to live on. But you must leave the empire without delay. You must apply for an exit visa tomorrow before the name Aquila comes to be linked with Quintus's."

Leaning forward, I reached out to him, but he just batted at my arms as if attacked by a colony of bees.

"Yeah, I'll sign." He half rose and then suddenly sat down again. "Hey, how do I know this ain't a trick?"

"Oh Binny, if nothing else, the money should convince you. You'll get half the ransom demand. Look, it's all explained in this document." I pointed with my chin to the scroll I'd been preparing on my desk. "Drusa has already agreed to sign it so she can keep her son and save herself from the charge of staging her own kidnapping. But you must sign it as well."

Squinting and running the tip of his tongue back and forth across his lower lip, he asked, "How soon do I get the money?"

"Professor Jason will have the document in his office tomorrow. You must sign it then. When you, Drusa, and I have signed it, he will notify the Bank of Gabinius to release half the ransom money to you, on condition, of course, that once you have the money and the exit visa, you'll leave. The rest of the ransom money will be released to Drusa and her son."

Focusing his eyes inward, he leaned back, rubbing his chin. And then the look of a hunted creature came into his eyes. "What about Gershon?" he countered, his voice taking on an urgency, his breath coming in snatches. "He knows I've been back. And Sergius does too."

I thought for a while looking into the darkness that was the peristyle and then spread my arms. "That's the chance we have to take. Gershon is a lumbering old man, and as for Sergius, he'd have nothing to gain by reporting you. In fact, he could face charges himself for creating a false identity for you.

"As far as I'm concerned, you died eight years ago in the Amphitheatre of Pompeii, and your body lies in our Jewish Cemetery. That's why you must never contact me or anyone else—especially Gershon, Sergius, and Drusa—and why you must leave the empire as soon as possible. Remember, the longer you stay, the more likely you are to be spotted."

With a flick of triumph in his eyes and an "I gotta go now," he grabbed one of the lanterns, charged through the peristyle, and leaped over the boxwood hedges. I wrapped my arms around my chest as I gazed out the library window and raised a hand to flash him a wave, but I'm sure he didn't see it.

He was gone, out of my life.

I stood there awash with relief, my eyes following his light along the side street as he began his run, the lantern rising and falling in a steady rhythm. While I watched, I allowed myself for one last time to indulge in the few sweet memories from our childhood: his teaching me to stand on my head, shinny up a tree, take aim with a slingshot, and land a punch. And then the speck of light disappeared.

Chapter Ten: Miriam

Despite my inclination to put the lanterns back and tidy my desk, I plopped into my chair and closed my eyes. Sinking into a glutinous sleep, I floated up only when pulled by a beam of afternoon sun and the aroma of mint tea.

"Good afternoon, Miss Miriam," said Calisto in a voice that rivaled birdsong. "I know you were up late with Mr. Binyamin, so I'm sure you haven't heard the news."

As I blundered toward consciousness, along with a cricked neck and a headache, my recollection of the night before trickled back.

"News?"

"About your brother."

"My brother?" I asked in a voice that was shriller than intended.

"The magistrate's soldiers were waiting for him—"

"What?" I tried to say more, but fear closed my throat.

She nodded. "They followed him from here and arrested him by the waterfront. They didn't want to make a disturbance here being that it was so late and the neighborhood so quiet. One of the soldiers, a special friend of a maid in the Valens Cinnus household—I met her this morning at Nestor's produce cart—said her lady sent for the magistrate as soon as you left her house."

So, Drusa betrayed him. I should have figured she'd want to keep all the money for herself. Besides, she could count on Burrus's contacts to support whatever story she'd concoct: that Aquila had kidnapped her, forced her to write the ransom note, kept her imprisoned in The Pegasus, and threatened to kill her. And when Quintus was slow to deliver the ransom, Aquila ambushed him, struck him with a blunt weapon, fracturing his skull, and perhaps while the old soldier was still gasping for air, dumped him in the lake.

I could figure out the rest.

Tears stung my eyes, but I reminded myself that I'd already mourned Binyamin's death. Aquila was an invention. So I walked out to the courtyard to feel the sun on my face and, in its fading light, watch the shadows lengthen until the pink and gold of the summer sunset drained out of the sky.

II

The Beggar

"I know nothing more worthy of a man's ambition than that his son be the best of men."
—Plato

Characters

- **Aspasia** owner of an apothecary shop
- **Calisto** Miriam's housemaid
- **Drusa** lover of Miriam's brother Binyamin
- **Elissa** slave and friend to Heset. They worked together in The Pegasus.
- **Fabia** hostess at The Pegasus before Selene. Nathaniel ben Ruben had been in love with her.

Chapter One: December 27, Late Morning

Something about the grizzly old dwarf begging in a splash of shade inside the agora's East Gate tugged at me. So, I called out to my bearers from the padded leather interior of my sedan chair to toss a coin into her collection box. Later I wondered what had prompted my charity. After all, the agora was throbbing with hordes of beggars, some tugging at my skirt, their pleas melding with the harangues of hawkers and hucksters, orators and priests, soothsayers and astrologers, tricksters and swindlers, magicians and conjurers, snake charmers and peddlers, wizards and sorcerers.

Perhaps she reminded me of the dwarf I'd met years ago at The Pegasus, a sleazy inn fronting the *Eunostos*, when I needed a courier to take a letter to Caesarea. The *Eunostos*, meaning the Port of Good Return, is the smaller and western of our two harbors and our port for exchanging goods with the cities along the Mediterranean. Surely I'd find a traveling merchant there to hire as my courier.

Like all the waterfront inns catering to sailors, roustabouts, and slaves, The Pegasus is in the *Rhakotis* Quarter, our district of poverty, pestilence, and despair, where most of the Egyptians live. When my bearers lowered the sedan chair near a sign depicting Pegasus as he sprang from Medusa's womb, I'd told them to wait while I inquired about someone heading to Caesarea. I then picked my way along a well-worn, dust-coated walkway beyond the street-front bar to the inn itself. Passing its façade decorated with a mural of Bellerophon on the white, winged Pegasus, I ventured in under its sagging lintels through a warped door that cut through one of the stallion's wings.

The inn's public room seemed empty that afternoon save for the ferocious flies in their metallic armor, the tang of putrefying garbage from the kitchen, and the stench of human waste from the latrine. But there, propped up on a wooden stool in the blind corner, dozed a bronze-skinned dwarf. He was leaning against a crooked wall, his weathered face lined with dirt, his chin sunk to his breast, and his graying Hebraic beard splayed across his chest. I cleared my throat to check whether he was sleeping, and in response, his eyelids fluttered, he scratched his little potbelly, and made a blubbery sound with his lips. Then, coughing up an oyster of phlegm, he opened his eyes and spat the slime into the chamber pot below his dangling feet.

Rubbing his eyes, he exclaimed, "Blessed be His Name! What's a fair maiden like you doing in a place like this? Or have I joined the World-to-Come?" The power of his voice and its mellow production of sounds belied his stature and our shabby surroundings.

"Excuse me," I said, "but I'm looking for an itinerant merchant to carry a letter to Caesarea."

"Nathaniel ben Ruben at your service," he said jumping off the stool, lifting his right hand from his heart to his lips to his forehead, and with a flourish, bowing deeply from the waist. "I'm to sail on the next Roman merchantman leaving for Caesarea so I can join up with a caravan headed for Jerusalem. Nowadays even Roman soldiers hiking along the most frequented highways travel in force to guard against an ambush by Judean terrorists."

When I gave him the address—I had to stoop to meet his gaze—he said, "I know the city well, having spent half my years trekking back and forth between Caesarea and Jerusalem."

So, satisfied he'd deliver the letter, I gave him the tablets, which he secured in a leather drawstring pouch under his stool. Bubbling with gratitude and filled with relief, I emptied my purse into his cupped hands, assured by his tattered cloak that he could use the money.

That was the first of my many encounters with that dwarf, Nathaniel ben Ruben.

Chapter Two: December 27, Noon

Rocking and swaying like a sailor on deck as my bearers nudged the sedan chair around moneychangers' tables, pushcarts, and awning-sheltered barrows, I felt that familiar thrill of being back in the heart of the city. Here in the cloaca of scandal and gossip, I was in the venue for seeing and being seen, for hearing and being heard. Like the legendary agoras in the Greek city-states, ours consists of a series of long, low buildings that face a central plaza, each building or *stoa* fronted by a portico to shade and shelter its shoppers. Within the *stoas* and their adjoining buildings are shops, small inns, and industrial workshops as well as cafés for light snacks and cookshops for a wider fare.

My husband Judah, the love of my life and Alexandria's jeweler extraordinaire, sent me a message this morning to meet him for lunch at Zenon's, a café that seasons the agora with the aroma of fresh cinnamon rolls. But his request pricked me with apprehension. First, his shop is busiest during the noon hour when streams of tourists, citizens, freedmen, and legionnaires pump through his shop. And second, he hinted at a question only I could answer. Had he stumbled upon a cryptic secret, perplexing crime, or baffling mystery? My specialties, of course, but whenever he finds out I'm working a case, he draws in jagged breaths as if the air had been cut into pieces. And his face darkens as his fingers rake through his glossy curls, still thick despite his forty-three years. So, I was uneasy rather than excited to be meeting him.

Zenon's is well-situated near Judah's *stoa*, which faces both the center of the agora and the Street of the Soma. Standing under the café's awning to escape the weight of the midday sun, I placed my order with the one-eyed counterman for a krater of pomegranate wine and two servings of their best *tiropita*, a multilayered pastry of phyllo and feta cheese. He must have just finished washing the tableware in the basin under the counter because as he nodded with an approving frown, he rubbed his thick, hairy hands across the long, once-white, grease-spattered apron that dipped below his paunch.

I crossed the mudbrick threshold into the low-raftered interior. Light leaking through the stained curtains behind the counter pasted a dull sheen on the sagging shelves of glassware, cutlery, and crockery. Then, slanting over the haphazard arrangement of chairs and tables, some butted together in groups, the winter sun washed the blue and green floor tiles depicting the strait between Scylla and Charybdis.

Taking a seat under the shadowed eave in the rear, I planted my back to the wall of gaudy paintings, all of men in a latrine, each scrawled with descriptive graffiti, some in verse, none leaving anything to the imagination. I drummed my fingers on the sticky tabletop while listening to the spikey jabber of hungry laborers on their lunch break and watching for that one pair of luminous green eyes to cut through the stew of faces.

And then he was calling to me as if he'd sprung out of the Earth. In the skin of yellow light from a smoking oil lamp suspended from a ceiling joist, I saw his face creased with concern.

"Hey Miriam. I thought I'd never find you," he said, his breath sawing in and out as he sank into the opposite chair and in that now familiar habit of his, leaned toward me.

As so often happens whenever Judah leans toward me like that, my memory takes me back eighteen years to the calends following my sixteenth birthday. That had been the day Papa asked me to start learning the investment business by collecting his mortgage payments in the agora. So that was the day I met the jeweler with the high-bridged nose and rugged cleft chin, broad shoulders and chiseled muscles, narrow waist and thickly lashed eyes. And that was the day as I was leaving that he'd leaned toward me for the very first time, close enough for our air to mingle. That sensation of his nearness would ignite my private adventures in solitary love and unleash a longing that was both mystical and earthly, passionate and tender, shy and eager.

The clatter of dishes, the chink of goblets, and the buttery scent of *tiropita* yanked me back to the present. A sharp-featured, walnut-colored youth was maneuvering through the maze of tables to serve us our order on Syrian glass plates with clutches of cutlery wrapped in Indian cotton napkins.

"I hope you don't mind," I said, laying my hand on Judah's arm. "Thinking you wouldn't have much time, I already ordered." I was about to unwrap the cutlery, but seeing his brooding face, I added, "Let's have some wine first" and filled our goblets.

Managing a wan imitation of a smile, he reached for his goblet. He took a few sips, savoring each before swallowing, and seemed to drift away for a few moments, perhaps to organize his thoughts. Emptying my goblet like a desert nomad, I held him with my eyes until I read relief in his shoulders and heard his breath fade into a sigh.

I refilled our goblets and waited for him to speak.

"It's Aspasia."

"Aspasia?" I asked, the pitch of my voice rising as I shook my head in disbelief.

Aspasia is the owner of the apothecary shop facing the public fountain in the *Bruchium* Quarter just west of the agora. Judah got to know her when she was his late-father Saul's landlady. During those last days, she would bring Saul opium to relieve his pain and cannabis tea to stimulate his appetite, strengthen his heartbeat, and relax his tremors.

I first met her when I needed her to direct me to Saul's apartment. Judah had asked me to assess his father's condition, although I knew from his description of Saul's cough that the poor man was suffering from acute mercury poisoning. Like so many other alchemists, he'd inhaled the toxic vapors while tingeing his other metals with its silvery color.

The memory of her neighborhood came back to me as a flash of images, its shops and saloons, inns and restaurants, tenements and warehouses, factories and grain bins, all jostling for space along the shoulders of the narrow lanes. Then I recalled the stench of the nearby *Rhakotis* Quarter, especially the stink of the canal that connects the *Kibotos* to Lake Mareotis.

When I'd knocked on the closed shutters of her apothecary shop, a frail-boned, old woman with a pleated mouth and liquid blue eyes squinted through the slats. Opening the shutters against the blazing daylight, she still gripped the long wooden key she'd used to unlock the grille, perhaps to have it handy as a makeshift club. In that glimpse inside her shop, I noticed an open scroll of *De Medicina* on her waist-high wooden workbench and behind it, a tower of marble shelves, each with orderly rows of containers labeled neatly with their contents. Likewise for the bundles of herbs hanging on ropes from her ceiling.

As we walked out to the street, she relocked the grille and closed the shutters. I followed her stooped shoulders and the yellowish-white braid straggling down her back as we rounded the corner of the building and passed through a walkway so narrow that I instinctively turned sideways until we reached a closed door toward the rear of the tenement. There she uttered a guttural rebuke to subdue the snarling mongrel that was chained to guard the entrance and led me into a dark stairwell that reeked from its own combination of urine, fried fish, *henket*, and something I couldn't identify. The smell intensified as I followed her hem up the steep, twisting staircase to the second-floor hallway where she left me alone to knock on Saul's door.

"Hey Miriam!" called Judah, snapping his fingers. "Did I lose you?"

"No, no, I was just thinking about Aspasia. I'm sorry. Please, tell me what happened."

"She was attacked. Happened early this morning. As soon as she opened her shop." Judah pinched his lips into a thin line. "By a woman, this beggar. Of all things, a dwarf. This thread of blood was still dribbling from the corner of Aspasia's mouth when she came running into my shop. She was screaming that her place had been ransacked by a dwarf. 'An uncommonly strong dwarf,' she said."

"Aspasia?" I asked again about this mildest of souls, made of only lightness, air, and sunlight. While I wagged my head in disbelief and uttered the usual platitudes, my stomach churned with the kind of relief that follows when the calamity is someone else's. "But she's all right?"

"Yes, yes but hey, I'm not done. I followed her back to her shop. That blood was now forking down her chin and leaking onto her tunic. I helped her cover the wound with a plaster of olive oil, honey, and lint. But the real damage was to her shop. So many amphorae smashed. And ceramic jars. Even the green glass vials on the counter. The porphyry counter in the front of her shop. All her tonics and medications. The castor oil, figs, and white hellebore; the opium; the aloe. Hey, you know what she stocks. Smeared all over the floor."

"What did the beggar want? She must have wanted something."

"Aspasia had been treating her for a fever and a rattle in her chest. Been giving her a potion to ease her cough and some opium to help her sleep. 'But when I examined her this morning,' Aspasia said, 'she hacked up this dark phlegm. Her *phthisis*, you know that deadly wasting disease, had advanced, but she kept pleading for a cure.' Aspasia said it was heartbreaking. But all she could do was explain that she had nothing for her. Only the medicine she'd already given her. Something or other made from licorice, mullein, and wild cherry bark. But the dwarf said it had stopped working.

"Anyways, Aspasia said that's when it happened. 'The beggar began to breathe convulsively—I was afraid she might die on the spot with her eyes flashing and her face burning with rage like that, but she threw a tantrum instead. It was fierce. She frightened me, stamping her feet, her nostrils so flared the edges turned pale. Then, when flecks of foam formed in the corners of her mouth, I knew I had to escort her out.'

"The beggar did not strike Aspasia, but when she flung the amphorae, vials, and jars off the shelves—it was her mad search for a remedy— one of the jars hit Aspasia in the face. Anyways, when Aspasia's blood started gushing, the dwarf ran away."

"Does anyone know where she went?"

He answered with a vague opening of his palms. "Well, of course, I stayed with Aspasia to clean up and put the undamaged containers back on the shelves. But hey, that's not why I sent for you. Something else happened. While I was sweeping her floor."

* * *

"Look, before you tell me about that, have some *tiropita*. You must be at least a little hungry. We can take the rest back to the shop and even bring some to Aspasia."

Flicking his hand, he shook his head, but then his face softened, and he gave me a barely perceptible nod. I unwrapped our cutlery and served us each a triangle of pastry, but he just rolled the cheese mixture around on his plate. Then, staring into his wine, he twirled the goblet in his hands and lifted it halfway to his lips before putting it back on the table.

"Okay, you've tortured me enough. Tell me what happened. You were sweeping her floor."

His brow creased in perplexity. "It's what I found. Among the shards."

"So, what was it?"

"A pearl." Except when he said it, he stretched out the vowels as if he were saying a three-syllable word.

"A pearl?" I asked, with a vague opening of my own palms as I shrugged.

"Hey, not just any pearl. A spectacular one. Large enough to cover my thumbnail. This perfect sphere, blemish free, and with an eerie luster. And that's not all. That rare black color. So that when you look at it closely, it shimmers with a deep purple color.

"I'd heard about such a pearl but never seen it. When I took it back to my shop—By the way, I didn't tell Aspasia what I'd found. She'd only worry that scoundrels looking for an easy fortune would ransack her shop and along with another mess, leave a dagger in her throat. Anyways I looked up the pearl in the codex. The one my father gave me. Says it comes from an exotic oyster. 'Very valuable.' That's what it said. And guess what else?"

He didn't even give me a chance to respond.

"The black pearl has the power to heal the brokenhearted and restore the health of the one who possesses it."

"So how did this rarest of pearls end up on Aspasia's floor?"

"Hey, that's what I wanted to ask you."

Chapter Three: December 27, Early Afternoon

When Judah unlocked the grille and folded back the shutters, his shop was unnaturally quiet, as if the appearance of this mysterious pearl had hushed even the flies.

"Other than the shards and smears, was Aspasia's floor clean?" The sound of my voice shattered the stillness as we entered his shop.

Judah's eyes opened wide. "Clean? You can't be serious." A pucker gathered on his brow. "What kind of question is that?"

"An important one," I answered with a cryptic smile.

We passed through the front of the shop where high-hung bronze lamps sprayed light onto his vitrines. Some of the cases displayed the presentation pieces he'd crafted in silver, gold, brass, and bronze: trays and platters, kraters and pitchers, candelabras and salt cellars, goblets and vases. Others artfully exhibited the commissioned pieces he'd fashioned: the signet rings and bejeweled chains, amulets and cuff bracelets, pendants and earrings, tiaras and brooches, many with complex mosaic designs, all expressing the taste and workmanship of a master craftsman.

Once we were behind the scrim that screens his office from the selling floor, Judah lit an oil lamp to supplement the watery slices of light filtering in from the louvered, east-facing window. By then, I was busying myself at the marble counter he'd built into the blind wall and the charcoal-burning cooking furnace he'd recessed into it. Grabbing a tin plate and some cutlery from the shelf above the counter, I unpacked the leftover *tiropita* from their strips of clean flax, set a few triangles on the plate, and placed it on a tripod above the still-hot embers.

"Hey, why are you asking me about her floor? Whether it was dirty?"

"Actually, whether it was gritty."

"Gritty? How could that be important?" Leaning his head back, he looked like he was searching the ceiling for an answer.

"It is if you want to find out where that pearl came from."

A smile formed in his eyes before it reached his lips.

"Drag that chair over to the table." I pointed with the serving spoon still in my hand to the one behind his desk. "I want to watch you eat while I explain it."

"Explain slowly. You know how distracted I get whenever you're near me."

"So, that's your excuse."

Another smile, this one like a beam of morning light.

And so we sat across from each other, Judah behind a plate of piping hot *tiropita* while I watched the light from the oil lamp brush his features with a soft glow.

* * *

"Remember that wind blowing off the sea yesterday? And how it must have keened against the buildings in Aspasia's lane? All I'm saying is her customers must have tracked in plenty of grit. So aside from the mess made by the dwarf, if her floor was otherwise clean this morning, she must have swept it before closing last night."

"So?" Judah managed to mumble around his mouthful. "She sweeps up every evening. She says, 'How can people have confidence in me as a healer if I look sickly or my shop looks grimy?' Anyways, at closing

I'd often go there. Something to get Saul through the night. Maybe garlic to ease his breathing or dill to settle his stomach. That's when I'd hear her broom scratching the floor."

He broke off the corner of another triangle of *tiropita*, popped it in his mouth, and rolled it around on his tongue. I waited for the ball of pastry to slide down his throat.

"So the pearl must have come into her shop this morn—."

He put up his palm to silence me. "Impossible. Only the dwarf came in. She couldn't have had anything like that."

"That's the only possibility, unless you think Aspasia dropped it herself. And if she did, she'd have told you to keep an eye out for it when you were sweeping her floor."

"Okay," said Judah, crossing his arms and leaning back. "So, how did this raggedy dwarf happen to have that pearl?"

I reached across the table for the rest of his *tiropita* and took a bite to buy some time before answering. "Well, we know of one dwarf who'd have a gem like that."

"Again, impossible." Judah shook his head while his tongue probed his teeth for a morsel of pastry. "Ben Ruben left years ago."

"Three to be exact."

"Knowing he could never return."

"And why was that?" I asked, knowing the answer full well.

"Well, for one thing, the murder of that civil slave. The one who lived in The Pegasus. The skulking jackal. Whatshisname? I just can't think of—Wait! Wasn't it Kastor?"

Fine for Judah to forget that schemer's name, but I never could. Kastor used to be Papa's secretary. Oh, he was competent all right if you could overlook his sly worldliness and malicious sidelong glances. He read and wrote Latin and Greek perfectly, but we ended up selling him to the civil authorities. We said my father was having financial reversals, but the strain on our budget was really because of Papa's gambling debts.

So Kastor left our household for a cramped, rat-infested *cella* in the *Bruchium* Quarter. After that, he was so spiteful that if I needed something from the Public Records Office, I'd send one of my bearers rather than have him wait on me. Anyway, he eventually moved into The Pegasus, where he was bludgeoned to death.

His murder was never solved, but ben Ruben remained the prime suspect because his walking stick was used to bash in the slave's skull and everyone in The Pegasus had heard them quarreling. And so, wrestling with frightful images of being arrested for Kastor's murder, ben Ruben moved out of The Pegasus. Because Kastor had been a valuable clerk, ben Ruben feared the Romans would subject him to the *summum supplicium*. He figured either the lions would feast on his flesh while flooding the arena with a crimson fog or he'd be crucified under a scorching sun accompanied by the drone of black bottle flies.

That was the irony. Ben Ruben was so terrified of being accused of killing Kastor, but even if he confessed, he'd never be arrested. To the Romans, Kastor was merely a piece of property. At most, the civil authorities could force ben Ruben to compensate them for their loss.

Ben Ruben, however, did kill two others, although their bodies were never found. He'd led each of them into the labyrinthine cellar of the abandoned warehouse where he'd hidden the jewels he'd recovered from the heist of the temple in Ephesus. All I can recall from the contents of the message he sent me is that he'd left one to rot there, the man he called the Brute, knowing the monster would die before finding not only the jewels but his way out.

The other was a crime of passion. He'd killed Fabia for spurning his love. In the beginning, he'd called her "our tarty, somewhat worn hostess of The Pegasus" and "our very own Venus." Later he referred to her as the shark he'd strangled as she rolled in terror, her eyes bulging, her face blackening, her tongue swelling, and her bowels emptying.

Still, at some point between those two remarks, she must have dimmed his eyes with sensuous pleasure.

"No, it wasn't because of Kastor that ben Ruben could never come back." Heaving up a sigh, I scratched my head as if that could help me explain what happened. "Remember when ben Ruben recouped the gems? He volunteered to return them to the people of Ephesus, and the priests here had a fête to honor him for his goodwill. Once the ports re-opened for the spring, Rome would be sending engineers to Ephesus to repair the city's underground pipes. So on the way, their ship, the *Minerva*, would stop in Alexandria to replenish supplies and pick up ben Ruben, his military escort, and the stolen gems."

I'll never forget that early spring day. Crowds had gathered at the Great Harbor to celebrate the *Minerva*'s departure. What a spectacle: a score of ships entering and leaving the harbor and pigtails of smoke wafting the odors of burning flesh from their pre- and post-sail sacrifices. We watched the military escort board the ship, but by the time the stevedores finished loading the supplies, ben Ruben had still not arrived.

I kept repeating in a voice as thin as a sheet of papyrus, "Don't worry. He'll be here," while I fought the bile surging up my gorge. And then we heard the blare of a trumpet, the shriek of a whistle, the groan of the ropes, and the whine of the hatches. And we saw the team of husky, sun-glazed rowers in the tugboat grab a line from the *Minerva*. Once they got her under tow and started pulling her toward the lighthouse, I was paralyzed with shock, knowing the ship was leaving without ben Ruben and the jewels. And the frustration of not knowing what had happened to him hung over me as if I'd swallowed a shadow.

"So, the Ephesians never got back their stolen gems."

"And I never stopped feeling bitter."

"Until now," said Judah, his face crinkling into a worried frown.

I waited for him to let out a calming breath. "Until now, when I know he's here, sick with *phthisis*, disguised as a woman, and pretending to be a beg—"

Judah began shaking his head before I'd even finished. "Hey Miriam, you're not going to look for him."

Of course, I didn't tell him that I'd already found ben Ruben. To Judah, ben Ruben has always meant trouble. Instead I said, "He was my friend, and now he's dying. He must have had a compelling reason for coming back, and I want to find out what that is."

And then to change the subject, I flashed him a wifely smile and said, "So show me the pearl."

Chapter Four: December 27, Late Afternoon

The grease from the cookshops hung in the air like islets of fog as I walked through the center of the agora, past the tents and awning-covered wagons filled with textiles from India, cheeses from Sicily, and copper pans from Gaul. I was almost back to the East Gate, certain I'd missed ben Ruben when I felt a tug on my skirt.

"Zemirah, is that you?" Whether because of his illness or to match his disguise, his voice was more like a feeble echo from the World-to-Come than the mellow production of sound I associated with him. But he was also the only one who ever called me Zemirah, no matter how many times I corrected him.

"Yes, it's me. Miriam."

Sitting on a boulder tucked in a polygon of shade, he was dimly visible as a stubby outline against a sidewall of the plaza. Rather than loom over him, I crouched in an uncouth squat along the razor line of a late afternoon shadow that split the cobblestones into light and dark.

"You didn't recognize me, did you?"

"No," I said. As the lie rolled off my tongue, I maintained the steady look that's indispensable to a good liar. I only hoped that my friend's features had dimmed in the minds of those he'd so bitterly disappointed.

I'd learned to fib and fudge, evade and hedge as a child when facing my father's accusations. My best performance was when, fixing me with a hard and searching look, his eyebrows pointing toward the bridge of his nose, he reproached me for seeing Judah. "Don't deny it, Miriam. I know you've been spending afternoons with that bastard." A stream of sour breath accompanied his bitter words as he leaned toward me. With his thick legs flung apart, his pupils dilated, and his jowls waddling, he stirred the air under my nose with his index finger.

In response, my eyes boring into his like gimlets, I planted my elbows on his desk. "Papa, Papa, Papa, Judah is just our client. I see him only on the calends to collect his mortgage payments." And he believed me, his favorite child, the one who grew to resemble the woman he forever mourned after childbed fever claimed her life and any tenderness he might have had.

Ben Ruben's cough startled me as he loosened a lung-full of mucus, retched up a blood-tinged clot of phlegm, and shivered before settling back against the wall.

"It's too dangerous for you to be here," I warned.

"*Shsh.*" He swiveled his head to make sure no one could be eavesdropping. Then, speaking to the pavement in a conspiratorial whisper, he said, "I'm here alone on an important mission, but come to think of it, I could use your help." Like a turtle, he withdrew his head into his hooded cloak while I nodded like a harmless idiot.

"Follow me to my new digs, even fancier than The Pega—" Before he could finish his quip, his budding guffaw had evolved into another coughing fit, this one expiring into a low moan that left a strand of spittle trailing from his lips.

The last time he'd invited me to follow him to his quarters was a few days after Kastor's death. Actually, we were interested in Kastor's room, which was next to his. Surely in a crime so violent, the murderer would have left blood spatters, even footprints, that could point to a killer taller than my friend.

Dressing myself as a prostitute was no challenge, but getting past Fabia to go upstairs was. That hawk-nosed, orange-haired hulk would sit at her reception desk, her chins slung like necklaces over her boxy shoulders. There she'd welcome the world with the cloying scent of cheap perfume, which hardly concealed the odors of sour bed linen, fermented semen, and flatulence that rose from her flesh.

But ben Ruben had a plan.

"Most afternoons immediately after lunch," he said, "Fabia announces she's going to the agora, but I know better. You can hear her entertaining one ship captain or another in her room behind the kitchen. If you dare go into the kitchen, that is." His mouth widened into a toothy grin. "Well, my room is just above hers, so I know what goes on. Her voice takes on a husky lilt as if her words could melt a stone, and whoever her companion happens to be, you can count on his words shredding the air with vulgarisms."

He lapsed in an embarrassed silence before continuing. "Anyway, Fabia left for the agora a while ago." He rolled his eyes when he said, "agora." "So we don't have much time, but I could take you upstairs."

According to ben Ruben, Fabia charges outside prostitutes a heavy tax for the use of her facilities. He'd rolled his eyes again when he said "her facilities." "Of course, if anyone else sees us," he added with a chuckle, "we could just pretend you've taken a special liking to me."

So to investigate Kastor's murder and clear my friend's name, I agreed to sneak up the stairs of that seamy, rat-infested inn with a man half my size and twice my age. He led me through a curtain of cobwebs to a steep spiral of narrow, warped steps. There the thud of our hurried footsteps filled the air to the second floor, which reeked of overflowing chamber pots and desperation.

I could only wonder what I'd encounter in his new quarters.

His meaty hands braced against the pavement, ben Ruben stood, his belly pressing the contours of his sweat-stained tunic as if he were hiding an inflated ball. With his collection box, walking stick, and ragged blanket in hand, he emerged from the shade, blinking like a cave dweller while I tipped a ragamuffin to run a message to Judah that I'd be late. Then I assessed my old friend's appearance in the amber light of that late afternoon.

He'd shaved off his lavish Hebraic beard, leaving only a few errant whiskers sprouting from his chin and a whiteish stubble that reached across his grime-lined face almost to his pouched, obsidian eyes. As before, sparse colonies of wiry hair flowered out of each ear and nostril, but the tangle of grizzled hair on his head had grown long. Some locks drooped below his earlobes; others shelved over his forehead where the flush of a fever had pasted a few snarls to his skin. Aside from that, his complexion was sallower and more pitted than I remembered.

Cocking his head this way and that, he listened for anyone who might follow us. After that, with a blueness about his lips and a hard swallow, he pointed his *calcei* eastward and pushed his belly forward like some extraordinary bird while our shadows streamed ahead to lead the way.

Chapter Five: December 27, Early Evening

I followed ben Ruben's heavy steps eastward through the teeming streets of the *Bruchium* Quarter, the city now awake after its mid-afternoon drowse. He stopped to rest or perhaps to gaze at a team of *pedisequi,* splendid in their white linen tunics and pigskin boots as they trotted ahead of their master's eight-slave litter to part the crowd with their long bamboo canes. Then they motioned the flat-roofed, fringed cabin forward to move like an imperial barge through the din of clattering wheels, bullying carts, and horse-drawn chariots.

Who could resist peeking in on the notables? For a moment, I saw a flame and was about to gasp when a more deliberate look showed me orange-haired Drusa folded into the compartment on an overstuffed cushion. Facing her was a boy, presumably her son given the torc of gold around his neck. Holding her head high and thrusting her chin forward, she graced me with a salon smile before disappearing behind a parade of peddlers hauling their handcarts. A fierce revulsion spread through me.

Adding to the hubbub of the *Bruchium* Quarter were swirls of sound: craftsmen hawking their wares, shoppers haggling, street philosophers preaching, and vendors peddling olives, boiled elephant beans, and honey-sweetened water. Even a platoon of soldiers taking a break from the weight of their cuirasses lay spilled across the roadway propped against each other with an intimacy known only to soldiers and drunks.

I managed to keep him in my sights except for a brief time when passing through a drove of pigs—and, oh yes, eluding that camel caravan. Skirting around limping matrons, awe-struck bumpkins, and overloaded delivery wagons, I trailed ben Ruben as he ducked and hid among the marble columns, arcaded galleries, and porticoed walkways.

The commercial neighborhood at last gave way to the gleaming façades of the marble, granite, and limestone townhouses with their tiled roof gardens, entrances decorated with ornamental lampstands, and lawns carpeted with rose petals. Soon ben Ruben turned northward toward the Great Harbor, the larger and more eastern of our harbors with anchorage for cargo transports, the imperial navy, and the private crafts of Roman officials.

Trooping behind him, listening to the tuneless twitter of birds returning to their roosts, I waited while he paused among the foundries, dockyards, and warehouses. Turning his head back and forth, was he getting his bearings, looking for that landmark known only to him, or merely gauging the hour by the lengthening shadows? In any case, he wrapped the blanket around his cloak. Then hiking up the edge so it wouldn't sweep the ground, he pulled a fold over his nose so he could breathe in his own warmth.

Watching him reminded me that the dying light would soon be asserting its chill, a development I usually looked forward to for its spicy coolness. But this time, I was filled with an immutable dread. So I drew in my himation and like ben Ruben, covered my nose to breathe through its soft fabric.

* * *

The evening came upon us all too soon. By the time ben Ruben beckoned me with a series of arm rolls down a lane that twisted into a narrow alley, the flare of the setting sun had turned the foliage to black lace. We passed the greasy windows of a lightless building sunk into the weeds, and there below a ledge, a flock of roosting pigeons snuggled together.

Just as I began to worry that he would never find his refuge, we came upon a crumbling stone warehouse leaning in solitude. As we passed through its weed-choked, rickety iron gate and made our way along the overgrown path, he withdrew a key from his purse. When he fitted it into the lock, the bolt slid back with a whine, and the thick oak door swung back with a groan. Perhaps it was those shadows creeping around me, but as soon as he opened the door, the air inside brushed my face with a whiff of death. *This must be the graves for Fabia and the Brute*, I thought with a shudder.

"Come in, my dear, and close the door behind you," he said, extending his hand. Claiming the lantern on its stand just inside the door and igniting the wick with the fire steel, he directed its melancholy beam into the low-raftered chamber. "Stay close," he warned. "If you get lost, you'll never find your way out."

I followed his trudge through an endless tangle of corridors, the walls a ghastly gray in the full light of the lantern. Holding onto the wall—like a tomb, it exhaled a fusty breath—I lowered myself down a flight of stone stairs, one clumsy step at a time. As the shadows quivered with the jiggle of his lantern, he led me through another tortuous labyrinth, this time to a fan-shaped cell, its cracked walls caulked with grime and furred with dust.

With a courtly bow, he announced, "Welcome to my palace."

I had to squat to enter his box of misery.

* * *

One wall was stacked with crates. Ben Ruben had appropriated a few and arranged them in a cluster to furnish his cell. He placed the lantern on a low box in the middle to peel back the shadows. Backing up to one crate, he levered himself upon it with his walking stick. Then he laid the stick across his lap, secured it under the shelf of his belly, and kicked the air with his stubby legs until he'd wriggled himself into position. Then with an imperious stretch of his arm, he invited me to do the same. Perching across from him, my eyes became accustomed to the flickering silhouette of his nose trembling in the hollow of his left cheek.

A coughing spasm ripped through him as if a pack of dogs were barking in his chest. When he finally caught his breath, I saw that he'd spattered his blanket with a murky sputum. Wiping a red smear from his lips with the back of his thick hand, he fixed his rheumy eyes on mine. Aside from their feverish burn and the scorched flesh around them, his forehead glistened with sweat.

A panic fanned through me. If anything happened to him, how could I get help, let alone find my way out? But after a snort through his nose and an extravagant sigh, more like a squall of wind, he began his story in a voice as hollow as an echo.

"Zemirah, thank you for bothering with an old friend, especially one who so publicly betrayed your trust. Rest assured, my pose as a beggar is only a front, one that enables me to cover my needs here and, at the same time, have an inconspicuous platform for gathering information. In fact, most of the gems from the heist remain. I've used this universal currency to support myself—but only in the humblest manner—and have likewise provided for those who, through no fault of their own, have had to depend on me these last few years."

"No worries, ben Ruben. After all, you were the one to carry my message to Caesarea more than a decade ago. And now I see that despite your illness, you've put yourself in danger by returning. Surely you've come back for a compelling reason."

My best friend and sleuthing partner Phoebe says I'm like a dog with a bone, that I never give up. But I was more than curious about what had brought ben Ruben back to Alexandria. I'd seen desperation in his eyes before and was afraid that if I didn't intervene, he'd do something bad, worse than in Aspasia's shop, something even deadly.

"I'm sicker than I thought, Zemirah." He cleared his throat to ease the whistling in his chest. "Perhaps I wouldn't have come had I realized that, but I expected to find a cure in the agora. When I first arrived— it was a few weeks ago, just before the ports closed—the apothecary gave me some opium and an herbal brew to ease my cough, but it did nothing for my fever. The opium helped me sleep, but when I got up, I was as weak as ever. And the woman in the apothecary—I think her name was Amalia—"

"Aspasia—"

"Yes, Amalia. She insisted she had nothing else for me."

By now, his voice sounded like it was spinning down a drain. His eyes had sunk in their sockets, and he was laboring to get his words out. "Maybe this Amalia—"

"Aspasia—"

"—thought I didn't have the money for a better treatment. Anyway, that's when I'm ashamed to say I got nasty. I made a mess of her shop while the poor woman stood there gulping in panic, and of course, I spoiled any chance of getting opium from her again."

Another percussive round of coughing left a sheen above his upper lip and a gout of blood on his blanket. "But sick or not, my dear, I came here to spy. At the time, I thought sitting by the gate in the agora would be the best way to gather information about my son."

"Your son?" I couldn't have been more amazed had he told me the emperor was his brother. My lips folded into a smile as I saw tendrils of pride spread through his chest.

"Yes, I dare say only this child—my child—he's named Yahya, meaning given by G-d—could have moved me to return to Alexandria. That, of course, and knowing that I don't have much time left to worry about the Romans anyway." He cocked his head to one side as a wry smile twitched about his lips. "So, my dear, I want you to find him for me."

* * *

Despite the trail of slime leaking from his mouth, the muscles around his shoulders relaxed, and he appeared to gain a spurt of energy as he told the story that began for him eight years ago.

"I met my son's mother, Heset, when I was living at The Pegasus. She was one of the slaves who belonged to Konstantine, the owner of the inn. She served him as a maid there. To earn money for herself, she worked in the evenings as a lady of pleasure. Perhaps we were attracted to each other because she too is a dwarf, but she is also quite beautiful, an Egyptian woman with sun-darkened, cinnamon-colored skin, thick dark hair, and black almond-shaped eyes."

"And your son?"

"Let's see." He bit down on the corner of his thumb and spat out a piece of skin before ticking off the years on his fingers. "I last saw him three years ago, just before I left Alexandria. He was seven then, still a child but reaching toward manhood. An obedient lad who swept the floors of The Pegasus every day. His eyes, round like mine, filled half his face. Otherwise, he was all angles." A chuckle of delight bubbled in his throat like a melody familiar from long ago. "His mother used to say he runs and jumps as if his legs are springs. And me? I'd answer that even when sticky with sweat, he smells like sunshine."

He stopped to dislodge something from his eye before flicking it away with his thumb and forefinger.

"When Heset told me she was going to bear my child, I was at first overjoyed, but then the idea that he'd be a dwarf, that he'd have to endure the same stings of mockery I've had to bear, haunted me." His voice dropped to a groan of bitterness so palpable that I felt it transfer to my own body. He recovered with a sad breath, but it took a little longer for me to win the struggle against my own secret tears.

"On the *Poseidon*, my getaway ship when I absconded with the jewels, I noticed this tall sailor gazing at me with an eager curiosity. Sometimes, his eyes would just touch me; other times, they'd embrace me. But they always fixed on me with an inquisitive gaze before snapping back to a safe place." As if to relive those moments, ben Ruben rubbed his own eyes with his fingertips.

"About halfway into our voyage, he approached me. Once the night sky was visible above me, I'd make my way to the galley to warm my supper, a pottage of wheat, millet, and corn that I'd re-heat each evening long after the crew and the rest of the passengers had had their turn at the grill. I'd put my pan on one of tripods that stood above the troughs of flaming charcoal and bring the stew to a simmer.

"That's when he came in, knowing we'd be alone. But somehow I wasn't afraid even though I was carrying those precious jewels, some on my person, most hidden in my chamber pot, a trick I learned from that shark, Fabia." He muttered a string of curses while his face turned maniacal with hate. "Did I just call her a shark? She was more like a crocodile cruising the Nile, her eyes just above the water, her senses alert, gliding toward her prey—"

"*Ahem.*" I feigned a cough as I put up my hand to silence him. I had no way to measure how much time had passed, but I'd begun to feel its weight.

"Sorry, Zemirah. I still can't get her out of my mind, how she looked: those bulging eyes, that blackening face, still sneering at me, mocking me—"

"Please, just tell me about the sailor—"

"Did I mention his name? Tabnit, named for his Phoenician father. Anyway, where was I?"

"In the galley with Tabn—"

"Yes. As soon as he saw me, his face broke into a tenderness, and he blurted out, 'You reminds me of my father.' That's what he said. 'My father didn't have no beard, but he had the same bowed shoulders and swung his arms when he walked just like you as if he was paddlin' the air. Maybe I'm not explainin' myself good. I don't even knows why, but whenever I sees you, I thinks of him.'

"Forgive me here, Zamirah. I'm not trying to make fun of the way he spoke. But the more I listened to him, the more I began to speak that way too.

"I asked him, 'Your father was a dwarf?'

"He nodded. 'And my mother too.'

"At that moment, peace flowed through me like a tide. I had a vision of my Yahya growing to a normal height, and I tasted for the first time in my modest stew all the delicacies I'd ever imagined. Some nights, I feasted on stuff squab basted with fig syrup; other nights, on cold pressed duck served over glazed oranges."

My old friend threw back his head and, pouring out a rich, rollicking laugh, held his belly as he rocked back and forth on his crate.

"Of course, when I left, Yahya was still too young for me to predict his growth, but since meeting Tabnit, I've dreamed of my son towering over me."

"And what have you heard of them since?"

"Nothing. Remember, I left in a hurry. The harbor was swarming with merchantmen. I booked passage on the first one to set sail before the *Minerva,* any vessel to escape the reaches of the empire. And other than the message I sent you, I contacted no one for fear of being arrested."

Of course, I remembered that roll of papyrus. It had no mark on the seal and was delivered in a locked box I had to smash open. All I could find out was that it was sent from somewhere near the Indian Ocean.

Although no names were mentioned, it was obviously from ben Ruben. He apologized to me along with confessing to killing Fabia, trapping the Brute, and bolting with the jewels.

"So, you don't even know where Heset and Yahya are right now."

"Right. I left Heset with enough rare pearls to buy herself and Yahya out of slavery and settle somewhere, perhaps to start a business. That's why I need your help. They could be anywhere, and I no longer have the strength to find them."

He rubbed his forefinger under his nose and wiped it on the blanket.

"And the rest of the gems?"

"Whether or not you find my son, I want you to send the remainder back to the people of Ephesus. I don't want to meet my Maker with that sin still on my chest. Like I said, there's a sizeable treasure left. As soon as I arrived, I secured a private box in the Public Records Office. I'm sure you know where that is, inside the Palace of Justice. The name on the box is Nathaniel."

I punctuated his information with a series of nods.

"I have two tokens." He dug into his sleeve to fish out an ostracon marked with the box number. "Will you take it?" A bead of spit flew out with his question, and his eyes locked onto mine.

I needled my lower lip with the edge of my teeth and nodded. I knew his time was limited. His sallow complexion, that clay color with a yellowish cast, and the tightening of the skin on his face were undeniable precursors of death. Still, I was willing to take on his mission not so much as a last act of mercy but for his commitment to send the rest of the treasure back to Ephesus.

"And of course, use whatever funds you need to find my son. I'll be here waiting." He closed his eyes and bowed his head as if to say a little prayer. Then, raising his head, he said, "And now, my dear, it's time to escort you out and teach you how to find the way yourself."

He jumped to the floor and, sweeping the air, stretched his arms above his head to catch me as I sprang from my crate. That's when he showed me, knotted to the base of one of the crates against the wall, the beginning of a long string that, hugging the walls and tracking the stairs, ultimately connected to the lampstand just inside the warehouse door. I hadn't noticed it when he'd led me into the belly of the warehouse. The faint cone of the light he carried stared ahead with only a dirty glow against the gloom trailing behind.

"I see now!" I said. "Give me the lantern and you follow me this time to prove I can use the string. And don't worry, next time I'll be sure to bring my own lantern."

When we reached the door, I gave him back his lantern, and we exchanged the usual round of parting platitudes. Still, after a backward glance, the certainty that I was leaving him with only the squeaks of rats for company burrowed into my gut like a maggot. Otherwise, I easily slid into the keen night air. Reckoning by the constellations strewn across the seamless sky, I judged it to be the early side of midnight. I made it to the agora guided by the Pharos Lighthouse and hired a chair to take me home while ideas for finding ben Ruben's son snapped in my head like sparks.

Chapter Six: December 28, Morning

Just as the feeble light of dawn was edging the walls of my *cubiculum*, I awoke astonished to be in my sleeping chamber rather than in ben Ruben's fan-shaped cell. My head throbbed, and a metallic taste lingered on my tongue. Next to me, the fluttering of Judah's lower lip in synchrony with his slumbered breathing told me he was deeply asleep.

As the details of ben Ruben's problem came trickling back, I wiped the crust of sleep from the corners of my eyes and slipped out of bed. Already I knew what my first destination would be.

Calisto, my shy, light-footed housemaid, was waiting outside my door with a glass of mint tea. As its fragrant steam tickled my face, the liquid slid into my mouth, cutting through the coating on my tongue and sending a trail of heat throughout my body. I shivered and let out a grateful sigh.

Calisto closed her sloe eyes and bowed.

I took another sip.

"Do not disturb Mr. Judah, but please lay out a fresh loincloth, breastband, and tunic for me, perhaps the cotton one with the geometric border print and the *stola* and himation I wear with it. And ask Orestes and Solon to be ready with the sedan chair. Oh yes, and please prepare a few bundles of sesame cakes wrapped in vine leaves and some amphorae of honey-sweetened water."

I drank the last of the tea, looking at her over the rim, but before I could thank her, she'd bowed and withdrawn without even a rustle of her coarse woolen tunic.

Papa had bought Orestes and Solon ages ago to transport him through the city. I prefer Orestes, the plucky one with sparkling eyes and sledgehammer fists, whereas Solon is the phlegmatic one. His time passes more slowly than everyone else's. When they're not in our outbuilding buffing the leather cushions of the sedan chair or waxing its carved mahogany supporting poles, each is available as a manservant for Judah or as a handyman or bodyguard for me.

I rarely use the chair, preferring to walk instead, but I do take at least one bearer with me when venturing into the *Rhakotis* Quarter. I'd learned the hard way, when my left eye was pounded into a puff pastry, never to venture into that pestilential underbelly alone, certainly not after dark. In fact, the thought of the *Rhakotis* Quarter turned my knees to jelly.

So I grabbed the arm of the mahogany sofa in my sitting room and dressed by the setting halfmoon's feathery light as it filtered through the cypress trees outside my window. I was grateful I could count on Orestes and Solon to escort me that morning, but I hadn't counted on the lie I was going to have to tell ben Ruben later and how it would tug at my conscience.

* * *

As I walked from our portico to wait by the side street for Orestes and Solon, I welcomed the warmth of the rising sun. Once seated in the sedan chair, cruising high above the rancid odors spilling out of the gutters and the thunder of wooden wheels trundling over the cobbles, I was soon looking out at the waterfront, painfully bright against the shoreline in the bite of that cool morning.

We continued westward beyond the agora through the twisting lanes along the harbor, past its lumberyards, stables, slaughterhouses, and storage bins, all pressed together with hardly a slice of sky between them. Finally, after plodding through the seedy, litter-strewn backstreets around the *Kibotos*, the small, square artificial port inside the *Eunostos*, the bearers crossed over the canal into the *Rhakotis* Quarter. At last, beyond a maze of rutted hairpin alleys, a shadow resolved itself into that familiar sign depicting the white, winged stallion. And then, farther ahead, at the end of a foot-worn path, I saw The Pegasus, a ramshackle inn of moldering mudbricks crouched in solitude.

With no sense of how long I might be, I handed Orestes and Solon the sesame cakes and honey-sweetened water. Then, while they parked the chair in an island of skeletal shrubs and squatted under a greasy front window to watch over me, I pushed open the thick, graffiti-scratched door. A trapezoid of sour light followed me in.

* * *

The same stink from years ago—stale bed linen, fermented semen, and flatulence—punched me in the face. Except now it was combined with the smell of enough *posca*—that cheap, watered-down, sour wine—to make a dog sneeze. I stifled a gag and sent a silent apology to Fabia for having thought those odors belonged solely to her.

I crossed the sticky wooden floor under a low-raftered ceiling to approach the ferret-faced hostess behind the reception desk and a post-menopausal mustache. Her huge hand was pawing a bowl of salted elephant beans. Scooping up a handful and popping them into her prune-puckered mouth, she greeted me with a "Whatcha want?" as she sputtered flecks of mashed beans through the gaps between her teeth.

I waited for her tongue and forefinger to dislodge the pulp that had gotten caught on her few remaining teeth and she'd finish swallowing.

"I came here to speak with you. My name is Miriam."

"I'm Selene. That's *Miss* Selene," she added with a veneer of sophistication. "I don't give out no information 'bout my guests. My boss, the most wonderful man in the world, forbids it." She spoke haltingly, as if reciting the line by rote from a shredded memory she didn't believe. The words were carried on the stink of yesterday's drinking bouts and the slur of a few more gulps that morning, but her sidelong glances told me she had more secrets to sell than a pomegranate has seeds.

"I didn't come here to speak with you about a guest," I said, planting a bronze coin in her salt-smeared palm.

The coin vanished before my eyes. Perhaps she'd slipped it inside the tattered sash that threatened to shred whenever she exhaled.

"I came to find out about a woman and her son who used to work here. Maybe you know them."

"Maybe."

"A dwarf named Heset. She was a maid here. And her son."

"Heard of 'em. Worked here. She emptied the chamber pots. Boy used to sweep. Broom bigger than he was."

A sadness ran through me, but then again, Yahya would have been so young then.

"Left not too long after I got here. Don't know what happened to 'em."

"Was anyone friendly with them?"

She held out that same palm. "Well, she did have someone. Another maid. Older Carthaginian woman. Can't think of her name."

I pressed another coin into her palm.

"Oh yeah. Elissa."

"And where can I find this Elissa?"

Selena left a gritty smudge on the wall when she leaned back and raised her steepled hands to her lips. I was afraid she wasn't going to tell me, but then she did.

"During winter, it's slow here. Konstantine rents her out to a man named Zephyr. Souvenir maker. Casts those bronze statuettes in the winter of the Pharos Lighthouse and Temple of Serapis. Then sells 'em to tourists when the ports re-open."

"Where's his shop? You say I can find her there?"

"Next to The Lizard's Tail. Saloon just east of here. On the *Eunostos*, halfway to the *Kibotos*."

"Thank you, Sel—"

"That's *Miss* Selene. And I don't wanna hear no one saying you got it from me, you hear? *Ma Zeus*, that's all I need. Working my ass off for that cheapskate with 'im accusing me of gossiping all day. Of being der-ee-lict when I don't even know what that means."

"Promise," I said, jerking back, thinking her gnarled forefinger was going to jab at my chest the way Papa's used to do. But no, my lurch was just an impulsive reaction to that childhood memory. So I mimed locking my lips and throwing away the key and felt the muscles in my lower back unclench as I turned, passed through the door, and walked toward my sedan chair with my arms swinging.

* * *

As we headed eastward, the mid-morning sun sent its swathes of light into the gloomy canyons of crumbling mudbrick tenements that were pressed together like spectators at the games. Orestes knew the way to The Lizard's Tail. He'd been there with Phoebe when she was tracking down the courier who'd delivered the ransom note in my recent kidnapping case. I expected the neighborhood to be quiet, with the ports closed and the revelers sleeping off the dramas of the night. But I was wrong. Bruised women in rags surrounded by drooping webs of clothesline haggled for food or sat in doorways nursing their babies while scolding their half-naked children.

My bearers stumbled through warrens of washboard roads in twisting alleys, kicking up geysers of dust through lanes slathered with graffiti and clotted with rubble. Then, after a bewildering number of turns, the monotony was relieved by the tawdry brilliance of a saloon pressed between a wine shop and a souvenir store.

With Solon staying to guard the chair, Orestes escorted me into Zephyr's Bronze Works, the souvenir shop behind a plaster model of the Pharos Lighthouse. The stones in the actual lighthouse were seamed with molten lead, but in Zephyr's statue, they were smeared with pigeon droppings.

* * *

The sun washed the pitted walkway to the two or three steps up to the wooden door, its crossbeams studded with bronze. The door screeched open to yield the smell of wax and the heat of the cast maker's fire. Then, sighing closed, it left Orestes and me in a lobby dark enough to blind anyone coming in from the daylight.

"Shall I bring in the lantern, Miss Miriam?"

"I think we'll be okay," I answered with a shake of my head.

Seeing no one but hearing the clang of a mallet against stone and the hiss of a broom, I called out for Elissa. Soon enough, a pair of hurried sandals clacked against the wooden floorboards, and I was greeted by a chinless, dough-faced woman, her cheeks like bloated cushions. She was followed by a cock and his hens, which she shooed away with a curt shake of her head and an unconvincing threat.

"Ya wanna speak wit' me?" Her high-pitched words were punctuated by titters, which hinted at her being either timid or nervous.

"Are you Elissa?"

The proof was in her blush.

"My name is Miriam. I am looking for a woman and her son. You used to work with them at The Pegasus. Heset and Yahya. Selene told me you and Heset were friends."

Elissa inclined her head, a sign that she remembered them. But if she'd said yes, the mallet's rhythmic clang swallowed up her voice.

Orestes, sure now that I'd come to no harm, slipped away. Still, I knew he'd stay in listening distance, probably just outside. Sure enough, he left the door slightly ajar.

Just as my eyes were getting used to the darkness, Elissa opened the curtains, drenching the room with sunlight and beckoning me with an outstretched arm to take a seat on the bench along the side wall. I hoped she didn't notice my momentary reluctance to join a house gecko feasting on a nest of wasps. She too sat, her profile half-turned towards me, so I could see that her sun-browned face was oddly crooked and webbed with fine lines.

"What can you tell me about Heset?" I asked.

"We were friends when we worked together. Then somehow, she was able ta buy herself and her son out a' slavery, I think wit' the pearls Yahya's father gave her. 'Black ones,' she said. 'Worth a lot.' But Heset was afraid Konstantine would change his mind. He'd say Yahya would soon be big enough ta fetch a lot more than the pearls were worth. So they went inta hiding.

"I'd told her Zephyr was looking ta hire an apprentice and would likely hire Yahya and pay him enough ta support—"

I stopped Elissa with a raised hand. "It's really Yahya I want to know about. You see, his father is living near the Indian Ocean and asked me to find out about his son." My lies used to come out from stiff lips and a dry throat, but I've improved by putting as much truth as possible into them and never looking to the left. That could be a dead giveaway.

At first, Elissa's face turned into an inscrutable mask.

Her eyes roamed over mine.

Then they slid away.

"Can you tell me anything about him?" I prompted. "Like did he grow tall?"

She pinched her lips, bowed her head, and stared at a crack in the floorboards.

"Please Elissa, you must tell me. Yahya's father is dying. I promised to tell him before—"

Raising her eyes, she looked at me, shook her head, and swallowed hard.

God of Abraham, what is causing this poor woman to experience such unspeakable pain?

I waited, staring so hard that her face became two.

But her mind was focused on the past.

Her features convulsed.

Her face collapsed.

Her mouth stretched wide.

And then the floodgates opened.

Tears must have been lurking behind her eyes because they welled up and spilled out. Stiff tracks scalded her face as they trickled down, leaving a glassy trail. Her head sinking into splayed hands, she howled, gulping for air, crying without restraint like a child being punished.

My nerves screamed with anticipation.

At last, her wave of grief broke and ebbed.

Her shakes subsided, and her sobs eased into sniffs and hiccups before sputtering to a stop.

She took in a ragged breath.

And I blinked away the prick of tears in my own eyes.

Then she poured out her story as if she'd unleashed the torrents of an early winter storm. She told it in jerks and pauses, her grief mixed with the guilt of a long-withheld confession.

"What happened—" she stammered, "—all my fault—talking her inta staying here, so close ta The Pegasus. How could I be so stupid! I keep trying ta change the story, ta give it a happy ending, but somehow it always stays the same."

She put her hands in mine and clung to them as if to a lifeline.

Her grief leaked into me, numbing me with pity.

"I got Yahya the job wit' Zephyr. A good job too, with a space for him and his mother ta live in the back. And I knew Zephyr would've given Yahya his shop when he died. He had no sons. But Konstantine found out where they were. That they were close by." She threw up her hands in despair. "Maybe a roustabout living at The Pegasus spotted them in a cookshop along the waterfront and followed them here. Who knows? But I'm sure he was paid well.

"Anyway, Konstantine—"Despite the clanging, she'd dropped her voice. Her lips moved but with almost no sound. "I have ta be careful," she whispered, leaning close to my ear. "He's my master too. He said, 'The pearls must be fake. How could that bitch have gotten her hands on such jewels? No way!' So, ta teach a lesson ta all of us, he had the pair captured in the plaza near the *Kibotos.*"

Now her hands were twitching like branches in the wind,

And I could see the flames of anguish in her eyes.

"Ta the Romans, his act was a lawful punishment for runaways." Her voice thickened to a groan. "The soldiers stripped them naked and caged them under the hot sun wit'out even a drop a' water until they died like criminals slumped in their own filth. And then, when no one but the blue-green flies came ta claim their bodies, he dumped them in the canal. That was the cruelest part because wit' no funeral and burial, their souls have ta wander forever, never ta find a resting place."

My palm flew to my mouth.

"I didn't mean ta do it, ta make it so easy for Konstantine ta find them. But I did." Elissa sunk into me, sobbing. As we held each other, rocking back and forth, I smoothed her dark hair as a fresh surge of hot tears flooded my shoulder. And then, lifting her head, drying her cheeks with the sleeve of her tunic, she looked at me, her face so haggard that she resembled a ghost more than a person.

"Elissa, Elissa, Elissa," I said, my forefinger lifting her chin. "Your people understand death to be the doorway to new life. Let us picture Heset and Yahya not how they died but how they're living now in a kinder world."

As her face softened and relief seeped into her shoulders, I withdrew but not before leaving a silver *denarius* on the bench, the largest coin I dare to carry into the quarter.

Chapter Seven: December 28, Afternoon

I'd reached the end of my investigation. Regardless of the miserable results—I didn't even know whether Yahya was a dwarf—I had to report back to ben Ruben, a thought that left me palpitating with dread.

Orestes was sitting on the stoop just outside the door, his hand hovering over the hilt of his dagger. As expected, Solon was waiting for us in The Lizard's Tail. Since it was past midday, I sent Orestes to join his partner for lunch and place an order for me. When they were finished, they filled my satchel with enough bread, cheese, and figs for ben Ruben and me, along with an amphora of barley water for him and some honey-sweetened water for me.

I was far too anxious to eat though; all I could do was drink the water.

As soon as we were ready, we headed eastward with just one stop at Aspasia's for some opium in case ben Ruben needed it to sleep. Although it was still afternoon, the daylight had begun to fade into the phlegmy light of winter. Before long, we were skirting the Great Harbor, deserted now as if by a plague, with only the mournful harping of the sea battering its piers.

From a mist clinging to the surface of the sea, there arose the vacant faces of a woman and a boy, surely a mother and son. I held my breath while the specter moved with the current before melting away like wax before a fire. Then I felt my legs tremble under the folds of my himation and *stola*.

Arriving at the agora, we searched the east end for ben Ruben. When he wasn't there, we went directly to his warehouse, all the while fear lapping at my feet. I closed my eyes against the frightful images flying before me, opening them only when Orestes asked where the turnoff was.

They dropped me off at the door to the warehouse. It was unlocked, so I knew ben Ruben must be inside, perhaps even waiting for me. Resting my satchel on the stand, I lit my lantern with the fire steel and untied the string that would lead me through the tangle of corridors, down the stairs, and into his cell.

By the time I reached the second or third step, I no longer needed the string. I could track ben Ruben's location by the rattle in his chest and the stench of his illness. I took a moment before entering his cell to tell myself that there was nothing to be afraid of. Nothing at all.

He was dozing, covered with his blanket as he lay on that same crate. I put down my satchel and observed him. Since yesterday, his skin had turned waxen, his eyes had sunk more deeply into their sockets, and his lips had lost their color. I patted the lump his knee made under the blanket, but there was no response. Instead, he continued breathing with thick, wheezy gasps followed by long silences. I was sure each lungful was his last until another heave rattled up from his chest and proved me wrong.

At last, he turned to me with a hooded gaze, his eyes glassy with fever. He tried to speak, but only a bloody foam gurgled out. He hawked a splotch of slime onto his blanket and tried to sit up. Slapping the dust from my clothes and placing his hands on my shoulders, I grasped him under the arms and pulled him up to a sitting position. He was surprisingly light.

"Zemirah?" Leaning forward and turning toward me, he stared at me with unfocused eyes as if he were gazing into eternity.

"I'm right here," I said, folding his hands under the blanket again. His skin felt like a burning kiln.

But he gripped my own hand as if he were dangling off the edge of a cliff. And then, his voice feeble like an echo that had come a long distance, he sighed "Yahya" in a tone tinged with excitement. "Are you here to tell me about my son?"

I brushed away his question with a wave of my hand. "*Shsh*. I want you to drink this first." I uncorked the amphora of barley water, bent down, and inserted it between his lips. He sipped slowly, and as he did so, he beat his chest with his fist.

He signaled he was done by licking his top lip, wiping away the rill that ran down his chin, and handing me the amphora. Then he nodded off. In the meantime, I moved another crate next to his and set out the bread, cheese, figs, and opium along with the rest of the barley water.

How long he napped I cannot say, but soon enough, another coughing spasm awakened him. Retching up an opal of phlegm, this one thick with blood, he pulled himself up, the crate screeching as he shifted, and blinked his way back to reality.

With his sputum so dark, I knew he had little time left. Still seizing my sleeve, he pulled me toward him with convulsive strength.

"Zemirah, tell me about my son."

A rivulet of sweat drew a path down my back.

And then a cold wave washed over me.

The tension mounted as we stared at each other.

He was getting weaker with each passing moment.

But the time had come for me to tell him.

And then, in the pause of a single second, I knew what to say.

"I spoke to a woman who worked with Yahya and his mother at The Pegasus. She knew them before Heset used the pearls to buy herself and Yahya out of slavery."

The wrinkles on his forehead eased.

I squared my shoulders and continued.

"Now they're living near The Lizard's Tail, where Yahya is an apprentice to Zephyr, the owner of a souvenir shop. Yahya's learning how to cast those bronze statuettes Zephyr sells to tourists. He's so pleased with Yahya—he regards him like a son—he has none of his own, you see. Anyway, he told me he'll make Yahya a partner in the business and give it to him when—"

"But is he tall, Zemirah, not like his mother and me?"

"Oh, yes, yes, like a cypress tree. Forgive me, I should have told you that from the beginn—"

"Bless you, Zemirah. You… have done me… such a… kindness."

He was speaking now with long spaces between his words, but I could hear the peace in his voice.

"Wait. You haven't let me fin—" I was just warming up. In fact, the story was so good I was beginning to believe it myself.

He sighed. But it wasn't a normal sigh. It was more like a gust. Then a tremor traveled through his body, the light in his eyes drained away, and he was gone. Still on his face though, was the faint smile that curved his lips when I told him his son was tall.

I straightened his limbs, smoothed his blanket, and feeling the warmth still in his eyes, I closed his crinkled lids.

Chapter Eight: December 28, Evening

"You're quiet tonight, Miriam. Anything wrong?"

"*Hmm?*"

"I said you look like something's troubling you. You've hardly eaten." Judah leaned over and gently raised my chin with his forefinger. "And I happen to know that roast goose with the cook's white almond sauce is a favorite of yours."

"Oh, Judah, I had such a sad day."

"Hey, I'm here if you want to talk about it. And I promise I won't interrupt—"

"Ben Ruben died today.

"You were looking for his son, weren't you?"

"Yes. He died right after I gave him my report."

"Well, I'm sure his death had nothing to do with what you told him."

"Oh, it's not that. He'd been sick for a while. A long while."

"So, what happened?"

"I found my way out of his warehouse—I mean the warehouse where he'd been staying—and called to a soldier, and together we got his body. And then I went to the Jewish cemetery to arrange a proper burial for him, you know, with mimes, musicians, and professional mourners. Just like I did for Binyamin. The first time anyway. There won't be any mourners, just me, but I'll ask Phoebe to come, and maybe you could close the shop for a few hours—"

"—Of cours—"

"I know you didn't like him very much—"

"Hey, that hardly matters now."

I glanced out the window overlooking our side street and saw that the twilight had thickened into darkness.

"And something else," I added.

"Yes?"

"You remember the pearl you found in Aspasia's shop? That rare black one? The one you put in your safe?"

Judah nodded, but now his eyes locked onto mine.

"Well, ben Ruben was the one who dropped it during the scuffle in her shop. I'm sure of it. He keeps—I mean kept—well, it's still there, of course—a private box in the Public Records Office for the jewels left from the heist. Quite a fortune. He'd lived modestly, you know. Anyway…"

"Anyways what, Miriam?" Judah's squint sketched a fan of wrinkles between his brows.

"I want to return that treasure to the people of Ephesus."

"You what?" he asked, dropping his spoon and gripping the edge of the table.

"I know. I know." I patted the air down with my palms as if that could placate him. "Carrying it would put me at risk, but the treasure belongs—"

"Miriam, that's much too dangerous, even for y—"

I cut him off with an upward flick of my palm. "But Judah, I couldn't really trust anyone el—"

"Look Miriam," he said while folding his arms across his chest. "You'll get your way. Always do, and I support you, but with this…Well, just think about it a long, long time."

I tugged my lower lip and nodded as if he'd persuaded me, but ideas were already coming at me like gusts of wind during a storm. Then, raising my eyes and looking again out the window, I saw that our mythological heroes had once again taken charge of the night sky.

III

The Black Pearl

"When I saw the sacred house of Artemis that towers to the clouds, the others were placed in the shade. For the Sun himself has never looked upon its equal outside Olympus."
—Antipater of Sidon

Characters

- **Cleon** nephew of and assistant to the high priest
- **high priest** the warden of the temple of Artemis
- **Judah** Miriam's husband, an accomplished jeweler
- **Manius Acilius Aviola** governor of Asia

Chapter One: July 19, Noon

The first time I mentioned going to Ephesus to return the stolen jewels, my delicately handsome husband Judah said no. Well, to be more precise, he dropped his spoon, gripped the edge of the table as if he were going to fall over and said, "Miriam, that's too dangerous, even for you."

But here we were seven months later in Ephesus. We'd arrived from Alexandria only yesterday after a muted sendoff—nothing like the celebration three years ago when ben Ruben was supposed to have returned the gems. But to my relief, Gaius Caecina Tuscus, the prefect of Egypt, assigned us a military escort to protect the gems aboard ship. Walking along Marble Street from our guest quarters in the Terrace Houses, I was quick to note the locations of the Square Agora and Theatre before turning right at the stadium and passing through the city wall at the Northern Gate. There we welcomed the breeze like a cool balm as it swept between the mulberry trees that shaded us along the Sacred Way, the last three-quarter-mile stretch to the Temple of Artemis.

Giddy with the anticipation of seeing one of the Seven Wonders of the World and swollen with pride for having come into possession of the jewels and having the opportunity to return them to their rightful place, I let my arms slice the air with a rare lightness. I would have felt differently, of course, had I known that a macabre sight awaited us, and like a sudden fever, it would turn our celebratory visit into a baffling tragedy.

* * *

Located in a spacious park on the plain of the Marnas River and surrounded by a double row of lofty fluted columns, the marble temple is lavishly decorated with sculptures in high relief, some gilded, others painted in a wide variety of colors. We carved our way through thickets of tourists, stews of bodies sweltering under the glassy heat of an Ephesian July. Some flashing the colors of their native garb flitted around like butterflies. Others in turbans wreathed in silver and gold haggled in a host of languages with peddlers hawking mummy-like statuettes of Artemis. A goddess of fertility more than the hunt, Eastern more than Hellenic, their syncretic deity was born locally before even the Greeks arrived.

Each tread baked through the soles of my *calcei* as we climbed the endless flights of shallow steps to the landing between two pedestaled charioteers frozen in stone, the air shimmering in waves around them. They too looked like they could hear the whisper of the fountain below and watch the birds frolic in its iridescent arcs. And then the heat of the day surrendered as we reached the coolness of the pronaos, the Ionic columned portico. With a nod from the sentries guarding the temple, we slipped through the bronze doors into the quiet vestibule.

The unnaturally quiet vestibule.

"Hellooooo," I called out. "Anybody here?"

An echo and then a dense silence.

"Miriam, I told you we'd get here too early." With a look I knew so well, Judah closed his eyes and sighed in exasperation. "While we wait, I'm going to fill my globe in the fountain so I can inspect some of the gems that have been here all along."

"You really brought your globe?"

"Just the little one—it'll give me some magnification—and my scratch kit to test for any fakes."

My attention was absorbed by the receding clicks of his footsteps until I couldn't hear them anymore.

That's when I saw we weren't too early; we were too late.

In the inner, windowless *cella*, sprawled across the floor to the right of the altar was a shroud of white skin, the face-up body of the high priest, clutching his chest, his cane just out of his reach. We'd met him last night in their town hall, the *Prytaneion*, at the banquet held in our honor. That's when he invited us to meet him here so he could show us the fully restored treasury, the source of wealth for the city's bank, the wealthiest in the Roman world. With his head rolled back and his body arched, his once-luminous but careworn face, like a weathered sundial, was now contorted in a malignant grimace that curled his lips in a teeth-baring snarl.

"Judah, come quickly!"

His tired footfalls slapped against the marble as he mounted the steps.

"Give me a minute."

"No, I mean now! Hurry!"

With a ragged breath, I waited the great length of several seconds. Wondering at the possible connection between our visit and the enormity of what had happened, I retreated into my recollections of last night's party. I'd gotten as far as smelling the governor's fetid breath when Judah's swift steps interrupted any further unfolding of my memory.

"What's—Oh, no! Miriam, what's happened to him?

"That's what I'm going to find out. Give me a minute to examine his body. You check the treasury—off the vestibule, the door on your right. Make sure everything is locked up and in order."

"You sure you can—?"

"Just go!"

At that moment, something else caught my eye. Something on the floor. Near the column to the left of the horseshoe-shaped altar. Perhaps a cushion. Round. Why should it be there? Leathery. Gray with a black zigzag pattern—Yikes, it moved! Or did it? Yes, it began to uncoil. A rock viper, the most aggressive snake in Anatolia.

Despite the noonday heat, a thin chill stole over me before cementing into horror. Of course, I recognized this venomous creature, having studied its habits and habitat in preparation for our trip. And those facts came streaming back: It feeds on rodents and other reptiles, prefers rocky and well-vegetated places, and attacks humans without provocation. Moreover, its victims experience great pain. But perhaps most importantly, if encountered, one should back away slowly.

Well, that was not an option because it was heading straight toward me. I watched with fascination as much as dread at the wave-like motion cycling through its body: the lifting of its belly scales to pull forward and then their dropping against the floor to pull backward. Maybe more laboriously than usual on the slick floor.

I looked around for a tool, anything to give me an advantage.

Nothing.

I shivered like a frightened horse; my palms bloomed with sweat.

But wait. There it was. Almost in front of me. I bent down and grabbed the tip of the high priest's cane.

The viper's head was almost at my toes. Good. Just where I wanted it. I pressed the curve of the cane's handle against the back of its head.

Its body writhed.

Too bad, Rocky.

I grabbed the serpent's tail with my empty hand, outstretched my arm, and let the creature dangle headfirst. It expressed its rage with an oily stench that sunk into my nostrils.

Now guiding the handle of the cane like a hook, I caught its head in the arc and carried the wriggling viper at Olympian speed through the rear portico, the *posticum*, and the forest of double columns. Then with all my might and shouting, "Good riddance!" I threw it into its preferred habitat.

In other words, I did Rocky a favor. I just had to stop shaking and remind myself to breathe.

"Did you call? I'm in the treasury. Be right there."

"Yes," I lied. Judah must have heard me bidding farewell to the snake, but I didn't want to catch another I-told-you-so about the dangers of our trip. "Was everything in order?"

"Hardly," he said, frowning as he shook his head in disbelief. "Either this city is full of the most careless people in the world, or someone here is as stupid as a stone."

"What's that supposed to mean?"

"It means the chest was unlocked and wide open. The stones I inspected with my globe were good—not necessarily top quality—I could see plenty of inclusions—but based on my scratch tests, all were genuine. I sampled assorted types, emeralds, topazes, diamonds, and rubies from different layers of the chest. By the way, the ones we brought were all there, except the black pearl. That was missing."

"You sure?"

"Absolutely. There were plenty of other pearls, none black though, and none with a metallic luster. Most were glassy or dull and nowhere near the size of the black pearl."

"Please look again. Before we call for the sentries, I'll check the high priest's body for a clue as to how he might have died and whether he has the black pearl or the key to the treasury. Remember at the banquet, he told us he had the only key. That more than carrying out the religious functions—the other priests and priestesses did that—he was the *neôkoros*, the warden, the official responsible for the financial affairs of the sanctuary."

"Okay, but I doubt whether the pearl is in the treasury. Of course, it could have rolled…" His voice trailed off until only an eerie stillness filled the sanctuary.

* * *

To determine when the high priest died, I untied the sash of his bleached linen robe and pressed my lips to his abdomen. Still warm. But given the heat of the day, he could have died even a couple of hours ago. When I felt the inside of his wrists, however, and saw they were just as warm, I knew he'd died only minutes before we arrived. My conclusion was confirmed when I was able to open his mouth. Rigor mortis had not yet set in. Aside from the odors of feces and urine—I turned away and breathed deeply to free my nostrils of their reek—a sour stink, like milk gone bad, rose from his throat to tell me he'd been about to vomit when he died.

Upon further examination, I saw on his right forearm near the elbow, a pale oval patch with a dry, scaly center. What's more, another scaly patch festered on the bottom of his left foot, this one larger, with an abnormally red, irregular border. Leprosy!

Oh, no! Now what? Should I continue to examine him? Well, why not? He's dead, and his infection is still in an early stage.

His lesions were hardly noticeable, especially with his long-sleeved priestly robe, but perhaps that's why, with both his vision and the sensation in his foot likely diminishing, he needed the cane—"

Judah's voice from the vestibule interrupted my conjectures.

"Find anything?"

"I'm still scanning his body. You?"

"Nothing yet."

"Keep looking. It's too soon to give up."

Continuing to scrutinize the high priest's foot, I noticed massive swelling around a few red puncture marks that could match the fangs of a viper. Moreover, based on the agony etched on his face and the misery in the curve of his back, I knew the pain must have hit him like lightning and raced through his body like a wildfire. But the bite wasn't what killed him. Couldn't have so fast. Instead, his heart must have stopped because of his fear of the snake and his failing health.

My next step was to search his clothing for a cranny to hide something. Perhaps inside his loin cloth or in the seams of his robe. I was about to quit when I noticed his sash on the floor where I'd tossed it. And there it was, the key on a ring attached under a flap inside his sash.

But alas, no black pearl.

"Judah!" I shouted. "I found the key so we can lock up the treasury. But not the pearl. Have you found it yet?"

"I'm coming." Weary steps and then, "The pearl is gone." His face darkened as he raked his fingers through his hair. "I'm certain. But what does all this mean?"

"That's going to take a while to figure out. In the meantime, let's lock up the treasury, get the high priest dressed again—"

"I'll do that—"

"And I'll share what I know with the sentries before they bring him to the mortuary. Then I think we'll be ready to walk back to the City Center.

* * *

We walked back along the Sacred Way, each in silent contemplation, looking at each other occasionally but neither willing to break the silence. All other noises were swallowed up in the barbarous heat that plastered down Judah's glossy curls and sent beads of sweat trickling down my back like crawling insects.

I'd been eager to ask the sentries about the snake, whether a rock viper had ever found its way into the temple, perhaps for the shade or an opportunity to hunt. When I stepped outside the pronaos into that world of brilliant color, the air burned my lungs like a sea of fire. And then, when I squinted into the molten light, the reflections from their swords stabbed my eyes as if with the points of their blades. Weighed down by the heat in their red-crested helmets, enameled cuirasses, and woolen tunics, their sunbaked faces stared straight ahead as they marched back and forth along the landing between the silent charioteers. I interrupted the slaps of their army sandals when I approached the fat one, his belly like a pregnant cat's.

"You get vipers in there?" I asked, pointing with my head toward the pronaos.

He nodded, apparently without the energy to respond further, just as the other one, as skinny as a stray dog and with a twitch in his grin, leaned in to say. "Not since I been here." Then he went on to say how long he'd been stationed in Ephesus, after which he started to chronicle his entire campaign history. I was afraid he was going to invite me to meet him at the Dionysus, a dive on the southeast side of the Square Agora next to a brothel and near the latrine so he could continue his saga after his shift. But I cut him off with a raised hand and explained to both what had happened to the high priest.

By then, Judah's swift steps were descending the stairs.

Given that one indicated yes while the other said no, I accepted the yes as a remote possibility, but in my heart, with the high priest dead and the black pearl missing, I suspected Rocky had had a little help finding his way into the temple.

* * *

The canopy of mulberry trees screened my eyes from the razor-edged light as tunnels of leaves, silvered by the glare, fluttered before us. The sun had begun its slide toward the horizon, but the craggy peaks of Mount Pion and Mount Koressos pierced a sky still brassy with the day's heat. As we passed through the Northern Gate and approached the City Center, I could see their steep slopes pocked with crests of jagged rocks and tangles of dust-laden shrubs.

Ephesus is in the saddle between those two mountains, and of course, it's smaller than Alexandria. Otherwise its colonnades and galleries, fountains and monuments, statues and temples looked familiar to me. Emblazoned by the afternoon sun, their warm stones radiated sparks of color.

Passing the Theater Plaza, we continued down Marble Street to the South Gate, which Augustus had rebuilt as a triumphal arch into the Square Agora. Eager for the shade of its two-aisled, two-story *stoas*, we caught a glimpse of an equestrian statue of Claudius with his unyielding eyeless gaze and found a promising cookshop. We lunched on salted fish, cheese, and dried figs served with an indifferent pomegranate wine under the watchful eyes of Priapus. Frescoed on the back wall, he fended off evil with the bells dangling from his extended member.

Then we took a roundabout way to our villa. Down past the latrine, brothel, and tavern on the steep grade of Curetes Street, we ambled through the narrow streets lined with awninged shops and the ochre walls and red-tiled roofs of the windowless upscale dwellings of the Terrace Houses.

As we approached the end of Marble Street and our western *insula*, the apartment house with our quarters, Judah turned to me to ask, "Hey Miriam, do you think we'll ever learn exactly what happened to the high priest?"

"Well, we have layers of questions to answer first. Was his death simply an untimely accident? He'd opened the treasury in preparation for our visit, and then he died before he had a chance to close and lock it. On the other hand, perhaps his death was a homicide. But if so, then what was the motive? It doesn't seem to have been burglary because even though the treasury was left open, no jewels were tak—"

"Except the black pearl—"

"Ah yes, except for the black pearl, if indeed it was taken and, in fact, by the murderer. That's what I meant by layers of questions. And if the black pearl was taken, why only that item? Don't forget, the high priest still had the key. Presumably once he was dead, the killer could have found it." Of course, I didn't mention the snake to Judah, but the killer could have been frightened enough by the snake to leave with just the black pearl.

"Can you think of any reason the black pearl would have been taken? I mean aside from its monetary value."

Putting his index finger to his lips, Judah considered my question. "Only one," he answered as he threw that finger at me. "Remember, its value is considerable, certainly more than any of the other jewels. But to answer your question: When I looked it up, the codex said that a black pearl has the power to heal the brokenhearted and restore the health of the one who possesses it."

"Well, that could certainly be a motive."

"Look. We got here yesterday. All we did was go to the banquet as guests of the high priest. Can you think of anything happening there that might shed light on his death?"

"You mean, could someone have overheard that he was meeting us at the temple at noon and inferred that he'd open the treasury for us?"

"Sounds like a place to start."

Chapter Two: July 19, Late Afternoon

We both needed to rest, and I needed to reflect on the interactions during the banquet. So we returned to our twelve-room guest villa in one of six residences built in pairs on three terraces cut into the northern slope of Mount Koressos. Each villa had an upper story reached by an internal staircase, but visitors had access to only the first floor. After we climbed the stepped street to the first terrace, Judah unlocked our heavily studded, bronze-hinged door.

The entrance led into a colonnaded atrium decorated with exquisite frescoes in golds, sea greens, and reds. In addition, graffiti, including signed love poems and lists of everyday necessities and their costs, were scratched on the wall. On the far side, a kitchen with running water lay just beyond the latrine and bathtub. Passing through the atrium into the peristyle courtyard, we circled the *impluvium*. This sunken marble pool, fed by the figure of a nymph tipping her jug, was edged with padded bronze benches and planters of yellow field marigolds, white chamomiles, and crimson lilies. Off to the left, we passed two dining rooms: one with a table and chairs; the other, larger and more formal, with dining couches. Both had floors tiled in geometric patterns with small black and white stones. Our sleeping chamber, the *cubiculum*, was straight ahead, but my feet pointed to a small sitting area, an alcove recessed into the outside wall of the courtyard.

I filled my lungs with the scent of the freshly cut roses pluming from the waist-high urn set in a corner of the room. Then, after rearranging the cushions, I plopped into one of the two citron chairs that faced each other across a three-legged cedar table inlaid with jasper and ivory. The afternoon sun, by now more yellow than white, filtered through the *compluvium*, the open space in the roof above the *impluvium*, to bathe the room in a buttery glow.

"Judah, you coming?"

"Be right there."

The echo of his voice through the courtyard told me he was in the latrine; having one indoors was an unexpected luxury. The public utility network in Ephesus provides internal running water from the *Aqua Troessitica* system of aqueducts and removes the wastewater from the latrines.

"So, have you thought of anything?" Judah asked as he sank into the chair opposite me.

"Give me a chance. The images have to bob to the surface." Then I kicked off my *calcei* and gathered my legs under me.

I started by recalling my impressions of that last block of Curetes Street when, in last evening's waning light, we'd made our way to the *Prytaneion*. Tilting my head back but still unable to see the summit of Mount Koressos. Listening to the torch lighters refresh their staves with sulfur and lime. Hearing the gulls as their cries drifted up from the harbor. Observing the lizards rustle the dead leaves around us. Welcoming the sea breeze as it found the nape of my neck. Watching the sun turn the windows to brass and the statues to gold. And then, seeing the first stars salt the sky.

The *Prytaneion* had the look of a private residence more than a public building. Entering from the east through a three-sided Ionic courtyard, we passed an altar dedicated to Artemis and Augustus before crossing into the Forecourt. When I explained to Judah that this sanctuary was a way of honoring Augustus as a partner to their virgin goddess, he said with a chuckle, "Oh, the Greeks of Ephesus must have loved that!"

"*Shsh*," I whispered with an elbow jab, "You promised to be on your best behavior."

I'd hushed him just in time. Emerging from the portico were two men: the elder, with a pious smile and a deep-eyed gaze who introduced himself as the high priest, and then his nephew and assistant, Cleon, whom he introduced as our neighbor.

"Neighbor?" I asked, wondering whether he could be from Alexandria or perhaps Crete.

A curve played at the corners of the high priest's lips. "Cleon lives near you, in an apartment in the Terrace House—the mirror image of yours, in fact—but in the eastern *insula*."

Despite the high priest's cane and a slightly sideways walk, he moved with a dignity so unlike the young man who accompanied him. His nervous-eyed assistant led with his forehead as if on tiptoes, a natural gait I suppose given his wry neck.

The heat from the crush of bodies besieged me as soon as we shouldered our way into the portico and Cleon began introducing us to the countless curetes, the attractive young clerics from prominent families who hold their esteemed office for one year. By the time he presented us to each of the nine priests for Artemis, her single priestess, and the scores of priestesses for Hestia, scalding rivulets were soaking my tunic. By then, a wave of dizziness was sweeping over me as if I were stepping off a boat.

Aside from the curetes, we met a host of women in a rainbow of Chinese silks, their skirts rustling the air and their hems brushing the floor while their red ochre mouths clucked effusive greetings in perfect Latin. Alongside them were their prominent husbands, all but one of their names lost in the deluge. I remembered only the former senator Manius Acilius Aviola, now the jowly, farm-faced governor of Asia because he had the kind of pink face a child would draw of a pig.

Judah's shifting in his chair pulled me out of my recollections.

"Miriam—"

"I know. You want to hear about our standing in the breathless heat of the portico," I said, spacing out my words in a stream dripping with irony, "dizzy with hunger and overcome by the reek of sour breath mixed with perfume over sweat—"

Judah waggled his head and threw me a series of impatient hand rolls. "I want clues about the death of the high priest."

"It doesn't work like that. First, I have to set the stage in my own mind to capture all the details."

"Okay. Okay. Have it your way. You always do, you know." I didn't exactly hear what he said after the second "Okay". He muttered something and knowing him so well, I'm guessing at what he said.

"Where was I? *Hmm.* Oh, yes. I was recounting the interminable introductions, and following that, the last thing I wanted to do was nibble daintily at the food. What I really wanted to do was gorge with undisciplined gluttony, lick my fingers, and burp—"

"Oh, Miriam, you always eat that way!"

I cocked my head to one side and answered with an airborne cushion that nearly toppled the urn.

"Now I see what a temper you have!" Judah leaned back and pursed his lips in mock distaste. But then he took a breath and in a more serious tone said, "But really, what more do you remember?"

"Well, I'm up to the building now. The portico was not only the façade for this modest town hall, but it opened to the first room we entered. Lined with couches and punctuated with shrines to various deities, it connected through a door fitted with a large marble threshold to the second and smaller room, the banquet hall.

"And now I'm remembering a few more things: our being seated at the head table with the high priest, the governor, and Cleon, though he was hardly there, occupied as he was with waiting on our table."

"Ah, now we're getting somewhere."

"Wait. I still need to conjure up the room itself: the tables covered in bleached Indian cotton illuminated by brass candelabra; Oriental platters of olives, candied nuts, figs, and cheeses, with kraters of Falernian wine to start us off; and a cohort of slaves with their huge ornate fans nudging the air and shooing the flies."

Oh, how I wished ben Ruben were here! He'd have scooped up those nuts with his meaty hands, fished out the cashews, stuffed them into his mouth, washed down the crumbs with a gulp or two of wine, oblivious to its being the most renowned in the Empire. Then he would have sucked his teeth and wiped the rills running down his chin with the back of his hand.

I felt the shadow of a smile play on my lips.

"And Judah, remember most of the time the high priest spoke about the city's being the center of worship for Artemis and its responsibility for maintaining the purity of her cult. That she's brought great wealth to the city, especially during her festivals—"

"No wonder Persicus—"

My palms flapped open. "Who?"

"Paullus Fabius Persicus. Don't tell me I know something you don't. Anyways, when he was governor here, maybe twenty years ago, he wrote an edict about—"

"Your mind is like a trap! But yes, I remember that. The corruption among the high priests. Well, what can you expect when there's an elite class—"

Judah swept away the rest of my remark with a wave of his hand and leaned over the table. "Never mind the corruption. The high priest was so proud that Augustus had given the city the black pearl."

"You're right! And he told us that as the *neôkoros*, he alone was responsible for the treasury, that only he had the key. I can still see him sculpting the air with his fine, long-fingered hands as he spoke in that patronizing tone natural to all men of importance. He invited us to see the black pearl in its original position in the fully restored treasury, just as it had been before the heist. That's when he mentioned we should come at noon."

"So who was around then?"

"You mean when he invited us?"

"Yes."

"Of course, he could have told others later. *Hmm.* On second thought, there really wasn't time later. The banquet ended late, and after the closing speeches, our table was the last to get up and leave."

"Right. So I'm asking again, who could have heard him?"

"Well, the five of us. Except maybe Cleon, who spent most of the evening ferrying dishes for the high priest."

"But the governor wasn't there either. Didn't you see him slink up to Sophia?"

"Who?"

"Sophia, the priestess for Artemis." Judah raised his hands to trace the outline of a voluptuous woman.

"So you noticed her. And even remembered her name."

"I remember all beautiful women."

Well, he recovered from that slip.

"Of course, I noticed her," he continued, "but the governor did more than that. When she was about to leave, he got up to dally—"

"Dally?"

"Yes, dally. You know. What you used to do when you'd come into my shop."

I let that remark dissolve in the ether. "So, the governor *wasn't* at the table when the high priest invited us. Which leaves only Cleon."

"And when Cleon wasn't scurrying around fetching for the high priest, he could have been hiding behind the fans."

"Oh Judah, you're beginning to sound like a detective! But all we really have is the monstrous death of the high priest and the missing black pearl."

"I say Cleon is our prime suspect, but I promised the governor that tomorrow morning I'd appraise the gems we returned to the treasury so he'd have an up-to-date evaluation of the city's assets."

"So how did the governor get the key?"

"I asked him that same question. He got it from the mortuary. The undertakers found it while preparing the high priest's body. Anyways, it's the governor's job to act as the *neôkoros* until the boule designates the next high priest. The position is hereditary, so the boule merely makes the appointment official. But in this case, with the high priest having no sons or daughters, the governor doesn't know who the successor will be.

"But look, tomorrow is our last full day here. So I'm asking you to wait for me before looking in on Cleon."

Rather than make a false promise, I flashed him my wifely smile.

* * *

The more I thought about it, the more I began to agree with Judah that the high priest's death just when the treasury would be open had to be more than a coincidence. And then, the presence of the rock viper and the absence of the black pearl convinced me.

As for Cleon, his arrival around that time wouldn't have raised questions with the sentries. Or he could have entered through the *posticum* and surely would have exited that way. So I resolved to pay Cleon a visit while Judah and the governor were in the temple. With the prospect of finding the black pearl, I looked forward to surprising them both.

Instead, I was the one surprised.

Chapter Three: July 20, Morning

Judah left to meet the governor before the sun lifted its forehead above the city walls. I feigned sleep until I heard the door close. Then I got up, dressed, and waited on one of the benches for the first needles of sunlight to poke through the *compluvium*.

I didn't want to arrive so early as to awaken Cleon, but without a key, I didn't want to come after he'd left either. I was prepared to gain entry with my gold bracelet—and an outright lie. I figured I'd tell him I'd found it on our banquet table and wondered whether it was his.

Stepping out as the morning light leaned against the slopes, I heard the noises gather on Curetes Street—the din of carts, the pleas of beggars, and the quarrels of men. And I smelled the aroma of fresh-baked bread mix with the tangy body odor of men at work. Welcoming the warmth of the sun on my face, I crossed the lane to the eastern *insula* and knocked on the door of the apartment that was the inverse of ours.

Nothing.

I looked around thinking I might have the wrong door, but that apartment was the only one that corresponded to ours.

Could I have missed him?

I knocked once more.

Again nothing.

So I pressed my ear to the door

And felt it budge.

Whew!

I pushed in the door and felt the breath of the apartment brush my face.

Would Cleon have left without locking up? Certainly not if the black pearl was there. Discouragement clutched at my innards, but at least I'd gotten inside and had the place to myself.

Or did I? I heard something. A ragged sigh? A faint whistling?

Someone is here!

I tiptoed through the atrium and courtyard, my heart thumping like a frantic fist, my mouth as dry as sand, the blood fizzing in my veins, my palms greased with sweat. But other than a peculiar complex of odors seeping out of the larger dining room—not tallow wicks or ripe bedding, more like the essence of a barnyard—I noticed nothing in those gaping rooms.

Until I peeked inside Cleon's *cubiculum*.

His head to one side. Deep chest breathing. His mouth open. Saliva trickling between his parted lips.

A snort came from his throat.

A shiver of fear spasmed through my body.

But he stayed asleep.

With only this one opportunity to search for the black pearl, I examined first the courtyard. My eyes raked the floor, especially under the catty-cornered benches and in the gritty corners, and my hands lifted the planters, flecked with brittle weeds clutching at life in the hard-baked soil.

As expected, nothing.

He's hidden it somewhere. I just have to find it before he wakes up.

Venturing into the kitchen, I came across what I expected: ceramic jugs of wine and olive oil, terracotta lamps, a wooden measure, a kettle, basin, saucepan, colander, pitcher, mixing bowls, and assorted knives, all of bronze; and a tankard, a few dishes and some cups, all of tin.

But no black pearl.

The dining rooms were essentially empty, but in the larger one, I found against the blind wall two more jugs and, oddly enough, a bleached linen cloth tented over a crate. One jug was filled wheat, but that foul, sourish smell was springing from the other.

Inside, I could hear squealing, scratching, scrabbling.

I tilted the jug to peek inside

And lurched back.

Mice!

What on Earth for?

Surely not...

I knew I had to look under the cloth.

I took a deep breath to brace myself.

Under the cloth was a mesh cage with a latched lid. On its bottom was a bedding of wood shavings, stones of various sizes, and a bowl that presumably had held water. And there in the corner was an inside-out snakeskin. I reeled back in anticipation of a vindictive hiss, but upon a closer look, I saw that the cage was uninhabited.

I noticed two more things in the room. Behind the jugs and against the wall, I saw a snake hook and a *cistula*, the small basket Cleon must have used to carry Rocky to the temple.

And then a sharp voice from outside cut into the silence: "Mir-i-amm! Mir-i-amm!"

Oh no! Judah is calling for me. I'd better sneak out of here before he awakens Cleon and sees where I've been.

* * *

I darted around Cleon's building and approached our *insula* from Curetes Street while slapping the dust from my skirt and composing myself so I could enter our apartment with a wooden face. As soon as I closed the door—

"There you are! I've been looking all over for you."

Judah was in the kitchen rinsing out his magnifying globe and the tools in his scratch kit. Then he shook his hands to dry them.

"So, how'd you do with the govern—"

"I couldn't imagine where you were and got a little worr—"

"I wanted some toiletries for the voyage home—"

"Oh, I wish I'd known. I need some things too: natron and mouth rinse. So, what did you get?"

My lies lined up like gulls on a rock. "Nothing. They didn't have anything I liked. So different from our usual formulas. Even the salve with honey. Too much lint. The *anethon*—"

"The what?"

"You know. For an upset stomach. Too much gruel and not enough dill." I frowned for the theatrical effect but then was quick to change the subject. "But you got to see the governor?"

"More than that. We got done early. I gave him a complete inventory—without the black pearl, of course—but I noted its value in case it's ever found, which I doubt."

"Me too," I said. Another lie.

"But wait till you hear this: When I left the temple, I walked back through Curetes Street and decided to do a little detective work on my own. And guess what?"

"You realized you were hungry and stopped at that cookshop—"

"Not even close! I stopped at Aphrodite's Daughter—"

"Uh-oh, the brothel."

"And the Dionysus."

"The tavern next to the brothel? I hope you didn't do any business at the broth—"

"Well, yes and no."

"What's that supposed to mean?"

Judah spoke while drying his globe with the skirt of his tunic. "It means I learned a lot about Cleon. That he's in debt at both places, for his tab at the brothel and his gambling at the tavern, where he's not very good at knucklebones. At least he's still welcome at the latrine."

"*Tsk, tsk.* Especially when he's supposed to be a model of purity. I wonder whether his uncle knew."

"Good question but now I regard him as reckless and don't want us to have anything to do with him." Judah's tone brooked no argument.

"Not even the visit?"

He pursed his lips and waggled his head. "Especially the visit." He spoke in a clipped tone, but then his voice settled into a patient drone. "Just make a list of what you want, and I'll check out the other apothecaries. While you're waiting, you can start packing for us."

Another wifely smile.

But how could I leave without fulfilling my promise to ben Ruben? Without seeing all the gems, including the black pearl, returned to their rightful place?

Chapter Four: July 20, Early Afternoon

As soon as Judah slammed our door, I put my bracelet back on—I wasn't going to bother with that subterfuge again—and stormed over to Cleon's. I wanted the pearl—not his promise but the pearl itself—before our departure tomorrow. And I wanted him arrested for the murder of his uncle.

The hordes of slaves, prostitutes, loiterers, and beggars seemed to part as I crossed the lane. And once I reached Cleon's door, I didn't even knock. I just barged in, shouting his name above the hum of traffic below.

He ran to the door. "Miss Miriam, what is it?"

"I want that black pearl, and I want it *now!*" I stamped my foot for emphasis.

But I didn't need to. His eyes had already opened so wide I thought they were going to fall out. "What are you talking about?" His voice almost sounded sincere.

"I know you killed your uncle with that snake, and before I report you to the magistrate, I'm giving you this one chance to hand over the pearl and plead for mercy."

His jaw opened and closed like the mouth of a beached fish, but after a sputter of saliva, he was able to say, albeit with long pauses between his words, "*Ma Zeus*, take a seat." Then, with a wave of his arm, which shook like a branch in the wind, he ushered me into the courtyard.

The air still bore the scent of a barnyard.

We faced each other on catty-cornered benches around the *impluvium*. While he gnawed on a callus near the tip of his thumb, he gazed into the shallow water. Despite the coolness drifting off its surface, I could see sweat beading on his forehead and smell the onion-like stink of his fear.

I sat as if a block and tackle were pulling my head and shoulders toward the ceiling. "I need to know why you killed your uncle." I said it in a flinty tone, not loud but penetrating.

Cleon shifted on his bench as if on a bed of nails and spoke in a somber tone.

"Yes, I killed him—but truly, Miss Miriam, I never intended to." His shoulders drew in, and the weight of sadness lay on every feature of his face. "Oh sure, I got sick of waiting on him. 'Get me this and get me that'—in public no less—so humiliating and with no end to his demands. Still, I loved him. He adopted me after my parents were killed in the riot. I was just a lad when they ran into the streets to join Demetrius in his noble fight to defend our goddess. The last I saw of them was when they were gathering stones to join the mob surging toward the Great Theater."

His face darkened as he continued.

"The night before the banquet"—he looked down at his palm as if the events of that night were written there—"I want to be clear because everything after that is a jumble—Artemis came to me in a dream and told me I could pay my debts and save my good name if I acquired the black pearl.

"See, you must be pure to serve the cult. I am deeply in debt, so much so that if widely known, I'd be discharged that fast"—he snapped his fingers—"even though my uncle was the…"

The rest of his words were blurred in gulps and gasps.

"And then the next evening was the banquet. I overheard him tell you and Mr. Judah to meet him at the temple at noon. I knew he'd open the treasury for you—something he rarely does. So, I got there a little before and came in through the *posticum* to ask him for the pearl.

"But to my shock—and shame—he refused!" Cleon leaned toward me now, his palms turned up in disbelief. "With all those gems glittering in my face—enough to fill this *impluvium* and more." He pointed toward the water, touching a spot in the air with his trembling forefinger. "My own uncle—my surrogate father—turned me down."

For a moment, I thought he would crumple like a dying leaf. But no, he just took a sad breath, a deep swallow, and continued.

"I pleaded—by then, I hated myself. My desperation was mounting, and my voice was squeaking like a child's, but still he refused. Me, the son who never asked for anything but gave him a lifetime of service and loyalty." His tone was ragged now, his breath coming in snatches as a tear broke through his lashes and tracked down his face.

"First he said that if I coveted the pearl, I wasn't pure enough to serve the cult. That's when my mouth loosened into a false laugh because everyone knows that high priests have been skimming from the treasury since the beginning of time.

"Then he lectured me as if I were a dimwitted schoolboy. He said that the black pearl had been part of the treasury for seventy years, that since Augustus gave that pearl to Artemis, the city has experienced an unparalleled peace and prosperity.

"I continued to beg, repeating myself though I knew it was futile. By then he was just staring—his lips pinched together in disgust, that crease between his eyebrows getting deeper and deeper. That's when I got so frustrated that for the first time in my life, I felt like striking him. I never did, of course, but in that instant, I dropped the *cistula*, and my precious pet got out—"

"Wait a minute. You brought that loathsome creature with you?"

"Oh, I often took it with me—in its *cistula*, of course. I knew people would be frightened if they saw it. But it's my pet. I like to talk to it while I walk around. Even sing a little. And it liked the fresh air. You know, it never caused me any trouble before—"

I thought he was going to go on and on the way people do about their children, so I interrupted him again. "Please just tell me about the black pearl." Besides, his words chilled me how, in such a matter-of-fact manner, he could refer to that creature as his loving companion.

But he put up his hands to silence me. "Once the snake was out, I lost control over it. It would not come back to the *cistula* despite my coaxing. Instead, it headed straight for my uncle. I shall never forget how his features contorted, the malignant look that took over his benign face. His head jerked back. The very sight of the snake paralyzed him. But then his face turned toward me, full of horror and astonishment. His lips parted, and his eyes glazed with shock.

"When the snake bit his foot, he uttered a guttural sound as if he'd been struck by a ferocious blow. He clutched his chest, gasped for breath, and collapsed to the floor.

"And then his body became rigid, and his eyes turned to gelatin." Cleon flicked out his tongue to moisten his parched lips. "All that was left was my uncle's body and the stink of his bowels. But the memory of his death—so needless, so appalling for such a devout life—will spin around in my brain over and over, again and again, to haunt me forever."

I let him brood for a few minutes, twining and untwining his fingers, staring with a vacant gaze across the water before I asked again. "But the black pearl?"

"Oh yes, I was getting to that. See, when I arrived, it wasn't in the treasury."

"What do you mean?"

"I saw it but not in the treasury." Cleon stopped to massage his temples. "When the snake attacked my uncle, the pearl fell from inside his sash. It bounced off my pet's head before dropping to the floor, and then my snake swallowed it.

I gasped.

"Then, right after that, I heard you and Mr. Judah coming. So I grabbed the *cistula*, ran out through the *posticum*, but in my haste, I left the treasury open. I figured after you left, I'd come back with my *cistula* and snake hook, close the lid on the treasury, and bring my pet home."

Cleon frowned in silence for an elongated moment.

"Look, Miss Miriam, I had no intention of killing my uncle. I really thought that with all those jewels, he wouldn't mind giving me the pearl. But in the end, you see, I've lost everything: my pet, the black pearl, and my beloved uncle. And now I must leave Ephesus before his death and my debts catch up with me."

The corners of his mouth drooped, his eyes flooded, his head sunk into his hands, and rocking back and forth, he wept. Tears flowed through his fingers while my own heart thumped, and tears pricked behind my own lids. I let him sob till his wave of grief ebbed, till his moans quieted into sniffs and hiccups, till he wiped the drips from his nose with the sleeve of his robe and a crust formed around his eyes.

I patted his knee.

"Cleon, even though you didn't intend to kill your uncle, your actions led directly to his death. Neither you nor your uncle, however, was pure. You coveted the black pearl to restore your credit, but your uncle, suffering from the early stages of leprosy, stole it to restore his health. But I will not report you to the magistrate if you abide by these conditions: You decline the position of high priest if the boule offers it to you. And to redeem your soul, you serve out your life searching in the forests and caves of this land to bring food, comfort, and companionship to the lepers.

"The choice is yours. I admit there's little evidence against you if you're called before the magistrate, but as you say, the memory of your uncle's horrific death will otherwise haunt you forever."

He cocked his head and funneled his lips as he considered my offer.

I waited while the seconds crawled past.

In that stillness, his chin lifted, his shoulders relaxed, and his jaw slackened. With a slow nod and a sigh, the light of a new journey appeared in his eyes.

Chapter Five: July 25, Late Morning

"You didn't tell me your cousin Eli owned this ship."

Judah and I were sitting across from each other on massive, carved oak armchairs in the lavishly appointed guest cabin of the *Orion*'s deckhouse. After these four days at sea, with so little to differentiate them, I had only a vague memory of the creaks and groans as the tug dragged us through the maze of sailing ships laying at anchor.

"Eli's father, my father's second cousin, started the trading company so he could transport goods by sea between the Mediterranean and China. He was my Aunt Hannah's only suitor. But my father and grandfather objected to him, claiming that his laugh was too loud, his nose too long, his palms too damp, his cologne too strong, his hair too greasy, his manner too familiar, and his tongue too glib."

"Hey, that's a lot of objections. What do you suppose was their real concern?"

"They believed he was more interested in my aunt's dowry than her welfare, that he'd take her to distant cities along his trade route where they couldn't protect her, that he might even leave her there while attending to business in other cities."

"Speaking of attending to busi—"

"Was I?"

"Okay, not exactly, but you never explained what really happened to the black pearl. You've told me about Cleon, his pet snake, and the high priest's lesions, but I still don't understand why his uncle took the pearl when he did. I mean he had the key to the treasury. He could have taken it after we left. Wasn't he afraid we'd notice it missing?"

"Well, we'll never know for sure, but I figure he was desperate. He recognized his disease and knew its inevitable progression would mean disgrace, even the loss of his home. No doubt he'd been clinging to the hope that the pearl would be returned before his symptoms became noticeable."

"Right, right. But he had the key. He could have taken it anytime. Why right then?"

"My guess is he was overcome by his own longing. He saw it as soon as he opened the treasury. Perhaps he picked it up, even caressed it, and couldn't resist the temptation to keep it. Or perhaps he would've put it back, but Cleon's arriving through the *posticum* startled him. So, he slipped it inside his sash."

"Something else, but I don't think you know the ans—"

"You always bait me when you say that."

"Me? Really?"

"Really!"

"Well, why do you suppose Cleon confessed to you?"

"Oh that. He felt so guilty. Guilty, of course, because he was indirectly responsible for his uncle's death and the loss of the black pearl. But also because he felt ashamed of his debts, knowing that he'd violated the standard of purity for his position."

"What a tragedy. But right now I'm relieved to be returning to Alexandri—But listen. The helmsman's shouting that he's spotted the lighthouse."

We rushed out the door to the corridor along the gunwale. And there she was, our Pharos Lighthouse standing sentinel over the Great Harbor, our tapering, white stone tower, her fire burning like a brilliant star in the southern sky. As Judah draped his arm around me, I felt the warmth of his enduring love.

Glossary of Foreign Terms

ad Aegyptum (Latin) literally "by Egypt," meaning that Alexandria was not considered part of the Roman province of Egypt. Instead, Alexandria belonged to only the emperor.

Alta Semita (Latin) literally "High Path," a street in ancient Rome that gave its name to one of the 14 regions of Augustan Rome

anethon (Greek) literally dill, refers to a medicine for an upset stomach made with gruel and dill

Aqua Troessitica (Latin) a system of aqueducts in Ephesus

bibliopōleion (Greek) bookshop

Bruchium (Greek) The palace quarter of Alexandria, the most magnificent portion of the city

calamus (Latin) a pen made from bronze or more commonly from a reed cut at an angle and then split

calcei (sing. calceus) (Latin) shoes worn outdoors with covered toes and straps extending to the ankles, calves, or knees

calends (Latin) the first day of the month in the ancient Roman calendar

cantharus (Latin) an earthenware, two-handled drinking cup

capitium (Latin) a short, light chemise used as a woman's undergarment or for sleeping

cella (Latin) a garret room or mean apartment

Circus Maximus (Latin) literally "Largest Circus," a Roman stadium for chariot racing

cistula (Latin) a small box or basket

collegium iuvenum (Latin) a social club for training high-ranking males over the age of fourteen in the martial arts

compluvium (Latin) the open circle in the roof above the pool in the atrium

cubiculum (Latin) a sleeping chamber

curetes (Greek) priests and priestesses

curule (Latin) the standard design for any Roman chair. The curule chair was made with curved legs forming a wide X. It had no back and low arms.

De Medicina a first-century CE medical treatise by Aulus Cornelius Celsus

damnatio ad bestia (Latin) literally "condemnation to beasts," refers to a form of public execution for common criminals in which the condemned was thrown to the wild beasts

denarius (Latin) the standard Roman silver coin during the first century CE

doctores (Latin) trainers of gladiators in a gladiatorial school

Domus Augusti (Latin) literally "The House of Augustus". It is situated on the Palatine Hill in Rome, Italy. This house has been identified as the primary place of residence for Emperor Augustus.

Eunostos (Greek) literally "The Port of Good (Safe) Return." This smaller and more western of Alexandria's two harbors is the port of exchange with other cities of the Mediterranean, the interior of Africa, and the Orient.

henket (Egyptian) a cheap Egyptian beer made from barley or emmer wheat

Hestia (Greek) goddess of the hearth

impluvium (Latin) the shallow sunken pool in the floor of an atrium. It receives rainwater coming through the opening in the roof above it.

insula (pl. insulae) (Latin) apartment house

Khamaseen (Arabic) a south-westerly wind that blows over Egypt in March and April

Kibotos (Greek) literally meaning the "box". It is a small, square artificial port in the *Eunostos*.

lanista (pl. lanistae) (Latin) the owner and manager of a troupe of gladiators

libitinarii (Latin) arena slaves who clear the sand and cart off the dead between bouts

ludus (Latin) school to train gladiators

Ma Zeus! (Greek) an expletive equivalent to "Oh Lord!"

neôkoros (Greek) warden of a temple, i.e., its sacred officer

nones (Latin) the 7th day of a 31-day month; the 5th day of a 29-day month

Palatium (Latin) the highest part of the Palatine Hill, the centermost of the seven hills of Rome

pankration (Greek) a strenuous sport that combines boxing and wrestling

pantopoleion (Greek) a general store

pedisequi (Latin) the slaves who follow their master when he leaves the house. Typically, they would accompany his litter to secure his safety.

phthisis (Greek) the name Hippocrates gave to a wasting disease known now as pulmonary tuberculosis

posca (Latin) a cheap, watered-down, sour wine

Poppaea Sabina (Latin) Emperor Nero's second wife

posticum (Latin) a back door, especially the portico behind a Greek or Roman temple

praegenarii (Latin) the dwarfed, crippled, and/or deformed men who, using wooden weapons, mimic the gladiators to amuse the crowd

Prytaneion (Greek) city hall

pugio (Latin) the long straight-bladed dagger and auxiliary weapon a *retiarius* uses to slit his opponent's throat

retiarius (Latin) the type of gladiator using a net and trident for his weaponry

Rhakotis (Egyptian) the oldest residential quarter in Alexandria where most of the Egyptians live

rudis (Latin) the wooden sword that symbolizes a volunteer gladiator's discharge from his contract

sagina (Latin) barley stew, the staple of a gladiator's diet

saniarium (Latin) the chamber where wounded gladiators are taken for medical treatment

Sefer Torah (Hebrew) literally "Book of the *Torah*," a handwritten copy of the *Torah*

spoliarium (Latin) the pit below the arena where the bodies of slain beasts and gladiators are dumped to await mass burial

stoa (pl. stoas) (Greek) a long, low building with a columned porch facing the center of the agora

summum supplicium (Latin) the most extreme punishment e.g., crucifixion or thrown to the wild beasts

stola (Latin) a traditional outer boxy tunic worn by married women

tiropita (Greek) a pastry made with layers of buttered phyllo and filled with a cheese-egg mixture

Acknowledgements

I shall always be indebted to my academic mentor, Professor Jean Lythcott, for inspiring me to create Miriam bat Isaac in the image of Maria Hebrea, the legendary founder of Western alchemy who held her place for 1500 years as the most celebrated woman of the Western World. I continue to feel Jeannie's blessings on all my work. Moreover, I am grateful to Verena Rose at Level Best Books for her interest in Miriam's stories.

Every writer should have a family and friends like mine beginning with my twin sister and earliest reader, Gail Trop Kushner, who painstakingly edits all my stories. My long-time friend, Professor Lewis M. Greenberg, a scholar of art history and culture, zealously checks the accuracy of my work. My newest support comes from Betsy Oden and Rondavid Gold, who encourage me as they gently critique my work, and from my web designer, Len C. Ritchie of LR Website Design, the most patient man ever born.

And I thank my friends old and new for buying my books; inviting me to present my work at their book clubs, luncheons, and community fundraisers; and otherwise sharing their enthusiasm for Miriam's stories. And I thank you for reading *The Deadliest Returns.* I hope you enjoyed the book. Regardless, I'd be grateful if you'd post a review. Your opinion really does matter. I read the reviews assiduously to make my next book even better.

But most of all, I thank my husband Paul R. Zuckerman. He is always here for me. He believes in me, brags about me, and embraces my every goal as his own. In addition, I hope that Maria Hebrea, whoever she was, whenever she lived, and wherever she is, forgives the liberties I have taken with her life. May she recognize my profound respect for her spiritual quest and scientific accomplishments.

About the Author

June Trop has focused on storytelling her entire professional life. As a professor of teacher education, she focused her research on the practical knowledge teachers construct and communicate through storytelling. Now associate professor *emerita*, she writes The Miriam bat Isaac Mystery Series. Her books have earned a Readers' Choice Award, a Readers' Favorite Award, and praise from the Historical Novel Society. One was named a finalist for the Killer Nashville Silver Falchion Award, and another was recognized by Wiki Ezvid as one of the nine most riveting mysteries set in the distant past.

Living in New York's Hudson Valley with her husband, Paul Zuckerman, June is breathlessly chronicling Miriam's next life-or-death exploit. Be sure to visit her website at www.JuneTrop.com.

SOCIAL MEDIA HANDLES:

Facebook: https://www.facebook.com/profile.php?id=100044318365389

AUTHOR WEBSITE:

www.JuneTrop.com

Also by June Trop

Other Miriam bat Isaac Mysteries:
The Deadliest Lie
The Deadliest Hate
The Deadliest Sport
The Deadliest Fever
The Deadliest Thief
The Deadliest Deceptions